EAGLES VIEW MOUNTAIN

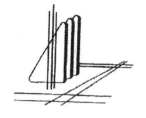

EAGLES VIEW MOUNTAIN

Civilization's Newest Explorers

Don C. Davis, ThB, BA, MDiv

Archway Publishing books may be ordered through booksellers or by contacting:

Archway Publishing
1663 Liberty Drive
Bloomington, IN 47403
www.archwaypublishing.com
1-(888)-242-5904

Cover inspiration by Nolan Davis

ISBN: 978-1-4808-1552-0 (e)
ISBN: 978-1-4808-1553-7 (sc)
ISBN: 978-1-4808-1551-3 (hc)

Library of Congress Control Number: 2015901956

Print information available on the last page.

Archway Publishing rev. date: 3/10/2015

ACKNOWLEDGEMENTS

A Place in the Story is the best of positive future-vision fiction, inspired by successful achievers.

Inspiration for my novel in seven sequels, *A Place in the Story*, has come from multiple sources, but none greater than from my wife, Mary, and our sons, Charles and Nolan, and their families. Mary, whose own success story continues to inspire her family, has been my devoted supporter and skillful editor. Along with these, there is the continuing influence of having loving parents who were good people.

The overview nature of my books has come from a list of writers whose books and articles explored the future, advanced knowledge, shared their knowledge base from science and technology, inspired positive insights, and led the way to a knowledge-based faith.

Those who have had a major influence on my thoughts and paradigms include: Norman Vincent Peale, Napoleon Hill, Albert Schweitzer, Og Mandino, Carl Sagan, Norman Cousins, Bill Gates, Fulton Oursler, Dale Carnegie, Theodore Gray, Norman Doidge, Martin E. P. Seligman, Michio Kaku, and others, whose vision is a reference to the future more than to the past.

From these, I have gathered an overarching view of the future. Like an impressionist painting, these provide a bigger picture of our place in the story for new tomorrows and the new sacred.

To: Dr. James Kelly *james/maria@crx.com*

From: Steve Kelly *stevekelly@crx.com*

Dear Granddad,

I can hardly believe what I am now writing to you in this email about my plans for this summer, but here goes. Dr. David Bergstein, my doctoral advisor, asked me to come by his office just two days ago and said, "I have an opportunity I want to offer to you." Then what followed his statement was almost beyond my imagination.

When I went to his office, he said, "I am a friend and colleague of Dr. David Logan, professor of International Studies and Social Policy here at the university, and guest professor at MIT each summer. He has a very unique retreat home on the top of Eagles View Mountain, overlooking the mountain town of Alpine. It's no secret that Dr. Logan has considerable financial means, which he shares generously. One way he shares is to make his retreat home on top of Eagles View Mountain available to doctoral students, working on their dissertation. Each year while he is teaching during the summer at MIT, a student is invited to live and write there. It's a wonderful place to gain perspective. So, I was thinking it would be a special place for you to work on your dissertation. I wonder if you would be interested in being his guest there this summer, at no cost whatsoever to you."

I responded in amazement. "Would I be interested?" I said. "Sounds too good to be true. But, yes, I would be interested!"

Dr. Bergstein said, "Okay. I will begin to make the arrangements immediately."

So, I have been packing up my things and the resource material I want to take and will be on my way tomorrow morning for the town of Alpine and Eagles View Mountain. Your books will be included. They already give an "Eagles View" perspective on life.

Perhaps there will be a time later when we could sit on the farmhouse porch and I could tell you all about my summer on Eagles View.

Your grandson,

Steve

CHAPTER ONE

Eagles View

*We read history backward but journey forward,
led by the way we enter new understandings of who we are.*

STEVE TURNED OFF THE INTERSTATE HIGHWAY AND FOLLOWED A STATE
road for three miles along winding mountain curves. Trees sur-
rounded the road so closely that each new upcoming curve was
barely visible. The road hugged the hillsides. Sometimes the steep
hills on one side of the road were matched by a sloping valley on
the other side. With homes tucked away among the surrounding
hills and so enshrouded by trees that houses were just barely visible,
one might easily be surprised that nine thousand people claimed
Alpine as the place they call home.

The atmosphere was pure mountain. Alpine had one major
street as its business section. The main street followed the floor
of an elongated valley. Some parts of the town showed signs of
recent development, but for the most part, it had the feeling of
being at its peak many years earlier. Even so, houses were kept
up as treasurers of pride. The thriving business district indicated
that the population tucked away in the hills enjoyed considerable
prosperity.

A mountain town had always held a measure of fascination for Steve. Now that Alpine was going to be his home for the summer, he drove into the town with open and elevated new interest. His home would not to be in town, but on the top of Eagles View Mountain. He had no directions except to go to Alpine and ask how to get to the top of Eagles View Mountain. After getting to the top, he was to go around the circle until he saw Lester Sawyer's name on the mail box. He would have the key to the house and would be the one he needed simply to call on for what he might need to move in and make it his summer home.

When Steve got to the town, he decided to stop at the first service station to get some directions. The middle aged man at the station kind of shook his head and said, "You sure you want to go up there?"

"Oh, yes, I'm sure. That's to be my home for this summer."

"Good luck," the station attendant said. "It's quite a climb."

"How do I get there?" was Steve's rather impatient request.

"Well, you go down Main street as far as you can before you have to cross the railroad tracks. As soon as you cross the tracks, turn right immediately and then follow that road until it bends left, goes up a steep grade for a short distance, before it takes a sharp right. That will be Cedar Mountain Road. At that point you will see the brown cedar shingled library and the fine arts and crafts center on the right. Across the road from that, and up on a hillside, you will see what once was one of Alpine's three thriving hotels. That was back in the good old days when people used to come up to the mountains on the train to spend week-ends or the summer. The old hotel is now an apartment building. Follow the road through a housing section, so heavily wooded that you can see only a few of the houses, and those not very well. Go about two miles and it will turn into Eagles View Road. Then groan your way up to the top. And I mean groan. Even with your 4 x 4 drive, that's what your SUV will do, groan. The pavement will end and after that the gravels will crunch under the tires. Lots of curves. It's quite a climb, but great mountain scenery all the way up. You got gas?" he said, as though his directions were complete enough to get the young stranger to the top of the world.

"Half a tank. I won't need any more than that, will I?"

"That will be plenty. But you may as well fill up. You may not want to come back down that often. Come back by here later and tell me how you made out. I haven't been up there in years. Never forgot the climb."

While Steve was filling his SUV with gas, he called out to the attendant, "Can I see Eagles View from here?"

Walking over closer, the attendant responded. "Oh, no. There are too many trees on the hills on each side of the valley. There is just one place you can see it. The town of Alpine more or less runs the length of the valley here, with business on one side and the railroad track running along the other side. So, if you want to get to that spot where you can see Eagles View, it will be at a church. To get to the church from here, go to where I said for you to cross the railroad tracks, but instead of crossing the tracks turn left onto Selvin Hills Drive. It leads up to the other side of the valley to a plateau area where there are lots of homes and one of the town's leading churches. In fact, it's the main church in town. It's where I go to church. There's a parking lot there that has enough space so you can see over the trees and see the peaks of the mountain range. Eagles View is the tallest peak of the range and the one that seems to kind of reach out toward town.

Some day you may want to scout out that side of the valley Go up past the church on Selvin Hills Drive and go on out until it winds through a kind of forest, then opens up into a big plateau area where there are lots of nice homes, the country club, and lots of small horse farms. But that's something you can do later. For now, you are probably only interested in finding your way up to Eagles View. As I say, good luck on the climb. You can make it okay, but it's quite a climb."

Steve extended his hand in a farewell, thank you, handshake. "My name's Steve Kelly. And you are?"

"I'm Harry Masefield," the attendant said, as he responded to Steve's extended hand.

"Thanks for your help, Mr. Masefield." Steve said, as he stepped away from the station and slipped into his SUV.

As soon as he crossed the railroad tracks he turned onto the street that turned steeply to the right and then to the left and up the hill. At the crest of the hill the street turned right. Across the street from the library and fine arts center stood the stately old hotel that Mr. Masefield had mentioned. He passed the old hotel and went up through a section of houses with elaborate front porches, as though they had been used in earlier years by people with lots of leisure time. Most of the houses were brown shingles or unfinished gray wood.

The winding road, that led up from the town of Alpine, curved past houses so hidden among the trees one barely got a glimpse of them even while driving slowly. On up the now steeper mountainside, the road was bordered only by trees and no houses. The paved part of the road ended. The curves were sharper and so close together that he was truly winding his way up the mountain, steeper and steeper. His SUV shifted automatically to its lowest gear and four-wheel drive. The motor groaned as the tires crunched the gravel. Why the people who lived up here on the top of Eagles View, chose that as a place to live may have indicated the identity they assumed for themselves, perhaps even their desire to get up to where they could be totally away - up to where they could feel the earth meeting the sky and the endless unknown.

It was springtime and the air was chilled by the spring air. Besides that, the cooler temperature went along with being up that high. As the road peaked, it intersected the circle he had been told about. An arrow pointed to the right to indicate it was one-way around the circle. Slowly he crept past houses which were on only the right side of the road, accessed by small driveways, winding among the trees, out to where each house overlooked the valley below. His car eased along slowly on the level road. He kept looking at the mail boxes where the private drives met the circle. The play on words was obvious on the wood-etched signs on each mailbox post, "John and Suzie's Eagle Perch." "The Sartins at The Top." Five houses later the name of the person from whom he was to get a key for Dr. Logan's house was on the mailbox. A little sign at the drive said, "We're Here. The Sawyers." The anxiety Steve felt by being so isolated eased a bit when he remembered that he had been told simply to find Lester Sawyer when he got here and he would take care of everything.

Steve turned onto the narrow drive and crept along, out to where the Sawyer house sat the edge of the woods and opened up to the sky and a view of the valley below. A knock at the door drew an immediate response as both Lester and Carlena appeared with big smiles and an immediate, "Welcome, Steve! We have been expecting you. So glad you're here. We want you to come in and visit, but we'll save that for later. Right now, you probably are just interested in getting over to Dr. Logan's, Look Beyond house." Carlena stepped over and said, "But let me give you a hug first. We welcome you. We are ready to help you out in any way we can."

She turned to Lester, who had already turned to go inside, and said, "Lester. Get the key off the mantle over the fireplace and let's go over and let Steve in."

Lester appeared with the key in his hand. "Steve, you can turn around here in our drive and then drive over. Carlena and I will walk over. We love to walk up here next door to heaven. We'll meet you there."

It was April and the air was chilly, almost cold. The wind whistled in the trees and the earliest of young leaves trembled in the chilled air. Steve reached back into the back seat of his SUV and pulled out his yellow sweater and put it on before he got back into his SUV to drive over to Look Beyond.

Steve turned off the circle drive and pulled into the driveway of the rustic mountain house where he would be privileged to live and write. He got out and followed Lester and Carlena onto the little back porch where firewood was stacked on each side. When Lester opened the door it echoed with a sound of isolation. But the warm welcome Lester and Carlena had given him made him ready to step inside and believe the "WELCOME" sign in big letters that was hanging on the brown door. The opportunity to live up here had all come together as a marvel. Up here he could have a place where his mind could be as clear as the fresh air and blue sky. Here he could overlook the valleys below as though he now held the undisputed right to reflect on the meaning of all he could see and his place in the story.

The house he was privileged to live in for the summer was one of a dozen or more homes perched on this little flat observation platform for retreat in the best sense of that term. Mostly the houses he had seen down each of the little driveways were made of unfinished wood with a rustic look equal to Dr. Logan's Look Beyond retreat house. As he had driven by, Steve could see that two of the houses were made of logs and occupied just as little of a footprint among the trees as possible.

The door Lester opened after he turned the key, was an entrance to into the great room. On the other side of the room was a big picture window and sliding glass door that opened out onto a long wood deck. Immediately it was inviting him to step across the room and look out through the window at the spaces beyond. "It's one of the best views up here," Carlena said. "Dr. Logan deserves a view like this since he's always looking out on the world with a searching sense of wonder. He sits out on the deck a lot with his coat on. Other times he finds refuge from the sharp cold winds by sitting at his desk table in front of the big window, soaking in the heat from the fireplace. You will probably do the same."

Climbing the mountain to such a chosen footprint had already done something for Steve's thinking. In his mind he thought, '*This is it. This is where I can gain perspective and feel the nature and the wonder of it all.*'

Carlena spoke with both kindness and assertiveness to Steve. "Now, Steve, don't you hesitate for one moment. If you need anything or have questions all you have to do was call on our cell phone. We have no land phone up here. We are here most of the time and ready to help. Dr. Bergstein from the university called to let us know the day you would get her, so there's a basic supply of food in the pantry and refrigerator. Lester has already set the thermostat, but he takes pride in keeping plenty of wood for the fireplace on the back landing." Lester pitched in and said, "Feel free to use it. There's plenty. You just let us know how we can help." They left their phone number, making him promise that he would call if there was anything at all they could do for him. "We will check with you later," Lester said. "Meanwhile make yourself at home."

After Lester and Carlena left, Steve stood at the table and looked out through the big window, savoring the moment. He reached down for the one thing he had brought in from the SUV. He pulled out his laptop and placed it on the table. Carefully and with a sense of the importance of what he would do here, he opened it. It only took a few moments for him to test the wireless connections. He was ready to connect his aloneness to the world beyond. It was a strange feeling. He had climbed up here to be alone and yet it was a place to see more than his aloneness. Musing to himself he thought, '*how could I ever have been so fortunate?*'

The deck on the other side of the window and sliding glass door was urgently inviting him to step out and look down and around. Steve stood with his hands resting lightly on the sun-bleached wood handrail at the edge of the deck. His eyes swept the panoramic view of the valleys below. Alpine stretched out like a microcosm of all the world's towns where people could live and have a place in the story. Except for glimpses, most of the town was hidden from view by the waves of green trees covering the mountains and valleys. He took a deep breath and savored the freshness of the cool springtime air, saying to himself, '*No wonder Dr. Logan likes to be up here on this pinnacle with its grand perspective. What a place to feel like you are looking out at the world and reflecting on life.*' Minutes passed before he took his hands off the rail and turned to go back inside to begin organizing for writing about the environment.

Back inside, he noticed a book lying on the table with a handwritten note sticking out from inside. Steve slipped the note out curiously. It was written by Dr. Logan. He sat down and began reading.

> **"Without having been told your name, I want to welcome you as my summer guest. And welcome to a special view of the nature of existence. All you see out the big window on the world is a result of the mysterious molecular activity of what is pictured and described in this book by Theodore Gray, THE ELEMENTS. I hope you will be able to read it as a framework and backdrop for whatever field of study you will be pursuing here, especially if it provides a cross-disciplinary view. We are a part of the molecular world which Theodore Gray has described and photographed in his marvelous book, and it is a part of us. We are civilization's newest explorers of the one hundred and eighteen known elements defined here. I invite you to become an explorer with me on a journey where we are discovering what we can do with what is given into our care. We read history backward but journey forward, led by the way we enter new understandings of who we are. As you read THE ELEMENTS think of us as colleagues. The book is for you as your personal copy.**

I look forward to sharing the journey together as new friends even though we have not met personally. Here is my email address. davidlogan@crx.com. You do need to feel you need to email me, but I will be pleased to receive it when the time seems right to you. Consider us as new fellow travelers on the leading edge of open-ended wonders, where all we ever get is a place in the story. It's where we can learn about, and be a part of the oneness of all that is."
James Logan

Steve sat down at the table and opened the book respectfully. *The Elements* would be the first book to read up here, where Dr. Logan was not only inviting him to share his retreat house, but to share a journey as an explorer of the nature of our existence. Steve thumbed the pages carefully before he placed it on the table and walked out on the deck again, reflecting on the mystery of all that is. With his hands on the wood rail he stared into the distance beyond.

He didn't know how long he had just stood there thinking, before he turned and went back inside. He opened his laptop on the table and waited for it to bring up the monitor. With his hands already on the keys he began to type as though it was a new page in a journal. He entered the date and wrote in pondering words, 'My Eagles View'

CHAPTER TWO

Venture Back Down

Our worship ought to lead us to be
open and honest as we shape our own story.

ON SUNDAY MORNING STEVE MADE HIS WAY DOWN THE STEEP AND winding road into Alpine to do what he had always done on Sundays, go to church. When he walked into World Citizen Church he was greeted by an usher, who reached out to shake hands with him and introduced herself. Clearly enunciating her name she said, "My name is Carol. Would you like for me to show you to a seat or would you rather be on your own. I'll be pleased to go with you," she said as she took one step in that direction.

"We are pleased you could share in our service today," she said, as she led the way through the open double doors leading from the narthex into the sanctuary. At the third pew from the back, she gestured and said, "Would this be all right?"

"This is fine," Steve said, as he accepted the bulletin she now handed to him. "Again, my name is Carol. You will be sitting with Martin and Sue Ashton."

When Steve was seated it was only a moment before Martin reached over to shake hands. "My name is Martin Ashton," he said. Then Sue moved over closer, and as she reached out to shake hands, she said, "I am Sue Ashton. We are pleased you have chosen to be here today. Here's a little card that has our names on it. If you would put your name on it, and other information that you don't mind sharing, and hand it back to us, it would help us remember. We're glad to have you visiting with us today."

Somewhat overwhelmed by such a personal welcome, Steve filled out the card, along with his cell phone number and summer address, and passed it back. Quietly they visited a moment together before the service began.

What Steve didn't expect was that as soon as the prelude stopped, the minister walked to the center of the chancel and said in her clear but rather quiet voice, "Good Morning." The people responded with "Good Morning."

"It's a great privilege we have today as we gather to explore the meaning of our growing faith. It's most likely we have people here who have come to be a part of this time together for the first time. We are pleased to have you with us. Remember, all of us were once first time visitors. But those who have greeted you are always glad to have an opportunity to introduce you to the rest of us. Who wants to begin?"

Martin and Sue Ashton were not the first, but soon they stood and said, "We have the privilege of sharing with Steve Kelly. We have learned that Steve is new to the area and is here temporarily, living in Dr. David Logan's retreat house up on Eagles View Mountain. He's doing some writing there. We are pleased to welcome him."

Others continued to introduce visitors. Already there was a sense of being in a relaxed and friendly network of caring friends.

As the minister ended the get-acquainted session she said, "Now, who are we?" The audience responded with three words. "Friends among friends."

After the service concluded and the minister was greeting people at the door, she shook hands with Steve, then went beyond the usual greeting and said, "We are glad to have you visiting with us today. I noted that you are living in the house that Dr. Logan shares with students for special studies. You may know already that Dr. Logan is much admired here, even though he is not here that often. I haven't met him yet. He teaches at MIT each summer and is frequently away on other engagements. I am interested in your studies here. Can you linger a moment until I have finished greeting the other people. Maybe we could go down to the office to share some ideas, or better still, we could have lunch together. And my name is Sandra Millan, she said, extending her hand again.

Responding to the handshake Steve said, "And I am Steve Kelly."

Her invitation seemed so open and sincere that Steve found himself saying, "Lunch would be fine. I'm open. But you may have family and need to be with them."

"Family? No. I am single. I am free for lunch. I would like that," Sandra responded.

Steve waited outside while Sandra went to her office and put her robe away. When she appeared only moments later on the walkway in front of the church, she said, "I am glad you agreed to have lunch together. I like sharing with friends at lunch. You may want to drive your car to the restaurant. So let's walk up to the parking lot and then you can follow me to the restaurant."

It all happened quickly and smoothly. Within fifteen minutes they were seated at a booth in the Home at Home Restaurant in the lower end of Alpine.

After the server handed them the menus, they began scanning its selections. "All the choices are good," Sandra said. "I am in here often. Cooking is not my specialty, especially on Sunday. Besides that, this is a place where I meet often with members and friends." After placing their order, Sandra began talking about Alpine and how fortunate she is to be privileged to live and serve here.

The talk soon became philosophical and Sandra was saying,

"Just because my undergraduate studies were in philosophy and social studies doesn't set me apart distinctively. In fact, the crossovers between those two ways of looking at things has helped me discover and explore new paradigms for understanding our oneness."

"Oneness," Steve put in, "That's a phrase my granddad uses a lot."

"Who is your granddad?" Sandra quizzed, interrupting what else he would have said.

"He is Dr. James Kelly. You may have heard of him." Steve said.

"You mean, the writer, James Kelly?"

"That's right," Steve responded.

"What a coincidence. He is one of my favorite writers. And he is your granddad!" Sandra said in exclamation. "I want to hear more about this. Obviously you have read his books."

"Oh, of course. And I have heard the stories in one of his books, told in person on the farmhouse porch."

Conversation was easy and open. Sandra talked about her getting the appointment to Alpine. "Like any student finishing seminary, I was at a crossroads. I could either take a church appointment, or I could do what I really wanted to do, go for my Ph D. In the end, I went for my Ph D. Then, having finished my classroom work, but not my dissertation, the opportunity opened up for me to come here. I put my dissertation into a holding mode and came here. No regrets. Finished my dissertation here.

But, back to your granddad's books. I was influenced by those books. Well, that's an understatement. Actually his writings caused me to do what he said he did, cross a bridge to an overarching knowledge-based faith and new beginnings. I took special notice of one line in his book. He said, 'I knew I had to look forward for my identity more than backward.'

So, what you saw this morning is a result of my decision to look forward and accept an appointment to Alpine. And I haven't regretted it at all. Alpine is such a unique and wonderful little town.

And such a good church. Wonderful people here. So, how do you like it here so far?" Sandra asked and waited expectantly.

"It's been only a few days, but I like it. Who wouldn't like it, getting to live up on Eagles View?" Steve responded energetically, but thoughtfully and said, "But, tell me. What does it mean that there is no cross on the altar at your church, just a figure of Jesus, as though he is standing on a raised rugged terrain with people standing and sitting around below, listening. It's obviously a representation of Jesus the Teacher. But that's quite different from what most altars are like, with an elaborate cross and candles lighted. It's a paradigm changer. What does it mean?"

"It means," Sandra responded quickly, "what was important about Jesus was not how he died, but how he lived, and what he taught. It means he was a human being, not just a thing that a distant and punitive God used as a substitute sacrifice to absolve people's sins. It means that it's more important to try to put the good into your life, rather than just trying to go by 'though shalt not,' rules to get rid of the bad. It speaks of a God down here, instead of a God up there. And it means that Jesus taught people about a kingdom of heaven they could work on in their own story. Does that sound like an explanation your granddad might have given? It should. I learned it from his books." Sandra said, and asked expectantly. "Am I close to being right?"

"You are more than close," Steve said. "He once told us the stories out at the farmhouse porch that present Jesus as a real person - someone who got dust in his sandals, but had the great ideas of a philosopher, with the dreams of a visionary in his head. The way Granddad told a story, you would think he knew Jesus as a friend - someone he respected for his openness and honesty. Unfortunately, the biographers let this down-to-earth understanding of Jesus get lost in the theological paradigm of those days, where they were looking for a sacrificial lamb, as in Jewish temple ceremonies, or for a Jewish version of Caesar. The images all get run together. Granddad would like your representation of Jesus the Teacher in the center of the sanctuary. As I said, it's a paradigm changer. What I can't figure out it is, how it happened, and how you were able to make that kind of change in a church. I would like to hear about it."

"How it happened," Sandra said immediately, "is that I didn't make it happen. The people made it happen. They were making some changes in the chancel and I will never forget the highly respected farmer on the committee, Clark Henderson. It has remained so vivid in my mind that if you don't mind I will run a little verbatim of what happened. Mr. Henderson said, 'the cross is overdone in the church. It's like as if I had to have a picture of my John Deere tractor everywhere out on the apple orchard farm - on my mailbox, on the corner of the house, on the tool sheds, on each door that once stabled horses, everywhere one can imagine having a picture of the main power unit for farming. Overdone. That's the word Mr. Henderson kept using about the cross.

He said, 'Many people don't like to see those tall crosses along the side of the highway - that it is far overdone. Well, it's the same at church. It seems to say the wrong thing about Jesus, and seems to be pushing religion at us, rather than sharing a faith with us.' Mr. Henderson became more outspoken than anybody at the church had ever heard him before. He said, 'People say Jesus died on a cross to atone for man's sins. Nobody knows that.' Clark Henderson could say that and get by with it. I couldn't have. He said, 'No angel ever came from wherever God lives to tell us that. People tried to make him a god like in Greek mythology, or make him the new messiah, a Jewish Caesar who would free them from Rome. Jesus flatly rejected those labels. What Jesus did accept for his role in his time was the simple idea that he was a teacher. He taught in the synagogues, in people's homes, from a boat, gathered disciples to go with him and taught them as they traveled. He was held in honor as a teacher. 'So,' Mr. Henderson said, 'Why don't we replace the cross, evoking sadness and sympathy - why don't we replace it with a depiction of Jesus as the teacher, sitting on a big rock on the mountainside, sharing his vision of how to live in daily life in a new kind of kingdom?' Mr. Henderson spoke quietly, but coming from him as a farmer, who still comes into town from his apple farm to be a part of the church – his saying that made people pay attention. It was interesting to see how people were listening instead of bringing up objections.

The discussion went on for a while. Then our resident psychologist, Vernon Lucas, entered the dialogue and said he liked the new idea, that it made lots of sense from his perspective. The discussion ended with their deciding to bring it before the Church Council.

As chairperson of the Church Council, Amy Emerson opened the meeting with the usual order of business and reports. Then she said, 'Dr. Vernon Lucas, has a special presentation he wants to make tonight. We all know Dr. Lucas as a trusted and respected psychologist here in Alpine. He has served our town and community for more than ten years since graduating from Sagan University, and then completing his Masters and Doctors degrees. He is not only a cordial and caring friend to us here in Alpine, but he is highly respected in his field of psychology in the university system across the state. Dr. Lucas very much agrees with what Clark Henderson says about the uses of the cross in the church. He came and talked with me about Mr. Henderson's idea. Then he met with Dr. Sandra. Upon her advice, he met with the Worship Committee.

'Now, Dr. Lucas,' Amy said, 'my opening the floor to you need not be as formal as I have made it sound. Come and share your ideas with us. Take all the time you need.'

'Thank you, Mrs. Emerson,' Vernon said. Instead of standing, he just moved a little forward in his chair. 'As Mrs. Emerson has already indicated, I live and work among you as a psychologist. In my counseling it is important for people to be open and honest. Very little therapy takes place unless both I and my clients are honest. And it's not easy to be honest. Most of the people I see as patients are looking for somebody else to blame for their troubles instead of being openly honest about themselves. And that crosses over into their religion where they also are looking for something to blame instead of just being fully honest.

Lest I fall into the same trap, I need to be openly honesty with you as my fellow members. When I enter this church Sunday after Sunday, I have a hard time with the dishonesty I face as I walk down the aisle. I am with Clark Henderson in what he said, about the cross being on the altar and in so many other places - that it's far overdone. And I am with what Dr. David Logan said one day. Even though he is away much of the time, I remember what he said once. I could relate to it. He said he wished he didn't have to turn both his cell phone and his mind off when he entered the church.

I have some of the same problem as Dr. Logan has. When I walk in my church there is the cross on the altar, representing an angry God who had no more heart than, as per traditional theology, than to send his son down to the earth to be born, live and die on a cross just to satisfy his own needs for justice. It's a visual statement about justice that claims sins must be paid for, or else the sinner will have to pay for them forever in eternal punishment. Who made God make that demand? Nobody knows. Himself? If that was the case, he could handle that all by himself.

The trouble with that paradigm is that Jesus didn't say that was the reason he was here. In fact he talked about something very different, about building a kingdom of heaven here in this world, not beyond it. That was his paradigm change. But when you look back on the main paradigm of religion in those days, it's easy to see that Jesus got squeezed into the traditions and mythology of that time, where gods came down and interacted with women, and from that the children born were gods, or emperors - super humans. Those identity images were not what Jesus wanted. This teacher in the synagogues talked about a down to earth identity where humble service is what counted.

However much one may spin it, a cross on the altar at the center of our sanctuary, represents an angry God who made Jesus into a thing to be used to pay for other people's sins. And that's wrong.

It's just plain wrong! That doesn't rightly represent Jesus, who prayed, 'forgive us our trespasses as we forgive those who trespass against us.' That puts forgiveness into something we have to do. It's our responsibility, or else it doesn't happen. We are accountable for what we have done. Our worship ought to lead us to be honest enough to face our own story. That's good psychology and that's good worship. That's when renewal and healing occur.

So, now, here is my open and bold request. Replace that cross, that symbol of an angry unjust God who demands subservience - replace that cross with a representation of Jesus as the Master Teacher from Galilee. Show Jesus standing on the mountainside teaching, with people standing and sitting below, listening carefully to his every word about how to live the good life and usher in a new kingdom. That's my simple request.

I know I look at things differently at times, but this is not out of character with how all of us were thinking when we decided to rename our church the World Citizen Church. That name calls upon us to care about each other - to "do unto others as you would have them do unto you," as our kingdom of heaven identity. When we come inside the church, the centerpiece of our identity can best be represented by a leader who asked of his followers, "love your neighbor as you love yourself." That kind of kingdom is up to us. Our identity should be shaped and reshaped by a renewed vision of who we can be when we are walking in the footsteps of the Master Teacher, who sat on a mountainside and said, "blessed are the poor in spirit," "blessed are the merciful," "blessed are the peacemakers," who said, "you are the light of the world...let your light shine so others may see your good works." He called on his followers to be a model. Jesus was that model, that teacher who prayed, "thy kingdom come, thy will be done on earth."

So, in place of a cross representing an angry God, we could have a representation of Jesus as the teacher, talking about wise ways of living that lead to being better people in the greatest time of learning in all of the human story.

Throngs of people followed Jesus as their esteemed teacher. They respectfully called him Master. His disciples understood that they were following a teacher. Jesus saw himself as a teacher. It's only fair that we respect who he thought of himself as being, and who his disciples understood him to be - a teacher. If we could have an icon on the altar that showed Jesus as the Master Teacher, such a representation could be created by a gifted artist who could be commissioned to create this honest paradigm for our altar."'

Sandra paused and said, "Steve, I know I have taken a long time to tell you about this, but judging from your intense listening, and how it parallels the way your granddad thinks, I hope you don't mind my doing so. What I have reported is not word for word, but it is a pretty good verbatim of what was said. But the next words I remember as an accurate verbatim. Dr. Lucas said, 'My interest in this paradigm change is matched by my willingness to take care of any cost that may be involved in finding and commissioning an artist to create that statuette of Jesus as the Master Teacher." He went on to say, 'That is my request and I await your decision.'

It was a little unlike Dr. Lucas as psychologist to do that much talking, so when he finished he slipped back into his chair and waited.

That's when Mrs. Emerson, as chair of the council, turned to me and said, 'Dr. Sandra, you may want to respond at this point.'

I paused a moment, then said, 'I didn't know I was going to have this opportunity. I am here to serve as both minister and leader. I can openly support Dr. Lucas' proposal. I am so pleased to be a part of a church that has turned loose of the past enough to embrace the future, as your new name indicates. So, I like what Dr. Lucas has presented to the council. But I think the better question is, 'Are all of you ready to be that boldly honest?' I have an openness to what is being presented, but the question and its answer belongs to you. So, yes, I do believe we need to align our answer to what it means to be the World Citizen Church, with the Master Teacher represented on the altar. So I say, 'If you ready to express this kind of bold openness, I am more than ready to support this new focus for our identity.'

So, Steve, they were ready. The church not only took pride in their new name as the World Citizen Church, but eagerly looked forward to a time when they could have the Master Teacher from Galilee represented anew in their church. They not only approved it, they could hardly wait for it to happen, and kept asking, 'When is the Teacher going to get here?'

The council approved the proposal and immediately Dr. Lucas began searching for a great artist to create the statuette. When Dr. Lucas found the artist they talked together at length about the way Jesus should be presented so it would be in character with who he was to his disciples. So the artist depicted Jesus like he is on the altar of the church.'"

Aware that she taken lots of time to tell the story Sandra said, "You didn't ask for this long explanation, but I get so involved in talking about the ideas that are a part of the story of this church I am privileged to serve that I hardly know when to stop talking. So, should I just stop here?"

"Not at all," Steve answered, and sat waiting for Sandra to go on.

"There was an open invitation for people to come by and see the statuette before it was placed on the altar. And when it was placed on the altar, they liked it even more. And I liked it so much. When I go into the sanctuary to meditate, as I do sometimes, I can almost hear Jesus asking me to talk about a kingdom of heaven the way he did, as though it's a dream in progress and a recurring call to quality-of-life living. That chosen identity is more important now than ever. I see myself as one who is supposed to be trying to make this calling real in my time and in my story. It has given new meaning to the pulpit where I stand week by week to be a spokesman for Jesus and his ideals in our time. You are right, it is a paradigm changer."

"Seems like a most unusual church," Steve said.

"It is," Sandra answered enthusiastically. "That may be the reason the bishop, who knew something about my progressive thinking, said that he had just the church he wanted me to serve. So he appointed me here. It's like Brer Rabbit being thrown into the briar patch. I was at home. And, you would be at home here if you are anything like the way your granddad comes through in his books."

"There is no doubt that I think like he thinks," Steve said. "He has had quite an impact on my life. And, even though I will be focused on environmental science, you may hear an echo of his talking in my dissertation that I am working on."

Sandra reached over and picked up the check the server had left much earlier.

"I will be glad to get that," Steve offered immediately.

"I know." Sandra said. "But let me get it. I hope we can talk again and you can get it then. Or, we can do better than that, we can do what helps to make for a good friendship – ask for separate checks."

CHAPTER THREE

When Theology Gets In The Way

*"It's gotten to the point that I can no longer keep quiet.
Maybe Martin Luther got to that kind of point
before he nailed his thesis to the church door."*

DAVID LOGAN LOVED TEACHING AT THE MIT DURING THE SUMMERS. It allowed him to live among, and speak with leading thinkers and innovators. It felt so right. He knew technology would play a significant part in a sustainable future. But he knew also that it needed to serve the best interest of humanity in order for it to fulfill a rightful place in the greatest time in all history. He liked the quick little dialogues he had with colleagues he had from time to time about that kind of focus on the future.

One Sunday morning he had just come from his frequent breakfast of bagels, juice, and coffee at the restaurant, when he met Dr. Craig Neilson, who was on his way to church.

After brief greetings, Craig said, "David, go with me to church."

Dr. Logan said, "Honestly, Craig, I have a hard time with most churches, so I rarely go when I am in Cambridge."

"I know," Craig countered. "I do too, but I go anyway. I just put up with some of it. Overall, I find something good about it. Go with me. It won't hurt you. Might do both of us good."

After they were greeted at the door at the church and given bulletins, they went up to the balcony. The organ prelude was filling the high ceilings with music that sounded like Bach's music. The bulletin listed the title as "Come, God, Creator, Holy Spirit." David began reading the bulletin while he listened and waited.

The choir processed as they sang, "Holy, Holy, Holy."

The liturgist stepped into the giant pulpit and said, "Good morning, and welcome to Christ Church on this beautiful Sunday morning." Leaving the pulpit, he walked to the center of the chancel, bowed before the cross on the high altar, then turned and said, "I invite you to follow the words in your bulletin and join in the Prayer of Adoration." Then he turned and faced the altar.

Dr. Logan followed the words, but didn't join in. He had already read them. He was in no mood to subject himself to that kind of servility any further by speaking the words.

> Holy God, to you alone belong glory, honor, and praise. We join with the hosts of heaven in worshiping you. You alone are worthy of adoration from every tongue to sing your praise. You created the earth by your power; you saved the human race in your mercy, and renew it through your grace. To you, loving God, Father, Son and Holy Spirit, be all glory, honor, and praise now and forever. Amen.

The elevation of God in such lofty language left Dr. Logan feeling disconnected and like a nobody.

"Let us join together in the Prayer of Confession," the liturgist said.

Once again Dr. Logan did not join in - just listened in disbelief that people would put themselves down by such degrading summations of themselves. He knew he was no saint by any means, but those words did not define who he had been trying to be all week. He listened.

> Most merciful God,
> we confess that we have sinned against you
> in thought, word, and deed,
> by what we have done,
> and by what we have left undone.
> We have not loved you with our whole heart;
> we have not loved our neighbors as ourselves.
> We are truly sorry and we humbly repent.
> For the sake of your son, Jesus Christ,
> have mercy on us and forgive us;
> that we may walk in your ways,
> and delight in your will,
> to the glory of your name. Amen.

Dr. Logan felt like a heel not to join in, but would have felt even worse if he had. Those words just were not true for him. He would have to lie to say, "we are truly sorry and humbly repent," just because he couldn't measure up to that kind of perfection. He felt betrayed.

A member of the choir came forward to the edge of the choir section and began a solo. He couldn't make out all the words but they were printed in the bulletin. He noted how much the words assumed that there is a transcendent God who expects all people to be obedient and servile servants, bowing down to his absolute will or else be subjected to his furry and punishment.

Dr. Logan's mind recoiled. It was an identity paradigm that was contrary to his understanding of humanity – that people make alternative choices which are the product of their thoughts and identity.

Dr. Logan thought, *'I have a problem with a big authority God who*

solves the world's problems by punishing everybody who doesn't comply with
everything just as he says, and only waives that sentence if they come to his
throne in servile guilt and beg his forgiveness in the name of a son, whom
he had sent to earth to get killed. That doesn't fit at all with a God of
molecular existence where cause and effect are linked in an ongoing marvel
of the behavior of every atom in all existence.'

When the preacher gave his sermon it was a rehearsal of the thinking from a thousand yesterdays. The assumption was that God made everything and then set up rules for how everybody was to behave, and if they didn't, they needed a mediator to plead for mercy and forgiveness on their behalf. The inference was that if he would let Jesus try his case before that heavenly court, he would win because it was God's own son that he had sent down here to set up a plea-bargain on his behalf. It was legal terminology, translated over into theology. The end result was, that by this defense he would be saved from God being so angry, and therefore he would not send him to hell forever to pay for his sins.

Dr. Logan could hardly believe what he was hearing. It was so incongruous with a real world where he, and his colleague sitting beside him, lived. He knew Craig would ask him about the service and the sermon after church was over. He would try not to offend him, but he knew he would have to be honest. His mind felt abused and trampled on. The perception of reality was distorted and defined by fantasy. He thought, *How could I be both honest and a diplomat?*

As he had expected, after church Craig said, "What did you think of the service?"

Dr. Logan answered in a quiet voice, "Are you free for lunch? We could talk about it over lunch." They drove down through the MIT campus and went into the grand contemporary hotel for lunch together. They both loved to eat there from time to time.

When Craig brought up the subject of the service after they placed their order, Dr. Logan entered a disclaimer by saying, "I don't mean to be critical of the service." Then he paused abruptly.

He caught himself in his attempt to be more courteous than honest and said, "Actually that's not quite true. In fact it's not true at all. I do mean to be critical. The liturgy was atrocious. I mean, it was so incongruous with anything we are thinking in our daily living that I was insulted to think I was supposed to listen seriously, as though that's the way the world works. Am supposed to leave church and go home feeling uplifted and ready to give my best in my time in history after being hit on the head with that kind of put–downs and theological contradictions? I would betray myself. I can't be honest with myself and do that. It's just not right."

They talked for an hour. Mostly Dr. Logan talked and Craig listened.

Finally Dr. Logan said, "It's gotten to the point that I can no longer keep quiet. Maybe Martin Luther got to that kind of point before he nailed his thesis to the church door. Anyway, it's so incongruous that I am ready to see what can be done.

I have divulged my feelings and gone on and on, without asking how you feel? So, how do you feel?"

Craig answered quietly. "I may not get as charged up as you, but I concur in all you have said. And it certainly goes counter to most people's thinking here at MIT. It counters and disconnects with the search for a better tomorrow. It makes the church out of sync with how we need to think in order to define who we are and can be.'"

Dr. Logan cut back in and said, "There ought to be a church somewhere that thinking people in our smart-phone-molecular age can go to without having to turn their brain off when they enter the door. And speaking of doors, I wonder if this is the way Martin Luther felt when he nailed his Ninety-five Thesis to the door of the church. I'm about ready to get my hammer and find a church door somewhere and begin nailing."

"Well," Craig answered rhetorically, "What about your church door? Of course, I don't mean that literally, but I've heard you say your church is very different. Maybe that's the place for you to start nailing - to speak up for the church you would like to see. But before you get out your hammer and nail, let me ask if you have read Dr. James Kelly's books, especially his fourth book?"

"Oh, yes," David answered quickly. "In fact, I know him. He's a good friend. I guess you could say that we think alike. He has different views too. Maybe that's why I see things so differently and get so bent out of shape when I go to some churches. Dr. Kelly is so different, so positive, so in touch with what's sacred in real time."

"He is that," Craig responded. "He defines faith in terms of the future. I have a suggestion, if you don't mind my giving it. What if you read his fourth book again? Then after that, get out your hammer and nail."

Chapter Four

To: **Dr. Sandra Millan** *sandramillanl@crx.com*
From: **David Logan** *davidlogan@crx.com*

Dear Dr. Millan:

I attended a church service here in Cambridge with a fellow professor this past Sunday and came away so dismayed that I felt totally out of step with the church. We went to lunch after church and talked. That's when I said, "There ought to be a church somewhere that you don't have to turn your brain off before you enter." My friend listened and said, "Well, what about your church? Why not share your thoughts with the minister at your own church." And every time I veered away from that he kept saying, "Welllll?" So I am sending this email to ask if you can give me some time when I am in Alpine again, to come in and roll over some ideas. Email me back at your convenience. If you are open to this, we can get together by phone to focus on a time.

Cordially,
David Logan

Reply

Dear Dr. Logan:

I would be very pleased to talk with you! Call me so we can set a time that works best for both of us. (412) 934-1022.

**Cordially,
Sandra.**

DR. LOGAN WALKED TO THE OPEN DOOR OF SANDRA'S OFFICE AND knocked lightly to announce his arrival quietly. "May I come in?" he asked, as he stepped in slowly.

"Yes. Please do, Dr. Logan," Sandra said, as she stepped out from behind her desk, extending her hand to greet and welcome him. "Ever since I came here I have heard about you. Now, it's a pleasure to meet you. I've heard enough about you that I am especially pleased to have this chance to talk with you as colleagues. Let's sit over here on the side in a more conversational setting."

"That will be fine," Dr. Logan said, "just as long as you remember that I am the one who is privileged to have this time you have given to me, and that you are the one in charge of the time frame."

"The time frame is open, especially since I have the rare privilege of meeting with you. Please, let's sit down together. News travels. I already know that you are away from Alpine most of the time and that you are at MIT for the summer. But here you are in Alpine now, and I am pleased we have this time to talk."

"It's always good to be in Alpine," Dr. Logan said. "This is a wonderful place. And I loved staying at the Bed and Breakfast Inn last night near here. Even though I haven't been here since you came, I have heard about you. And from what I hear, I already know we share some common journey in our thinking. As you say, news travels. I have read all four of Dr. James Kelly books and what I hear is that you have read his books. Very interesting, aren't they? All fiction, as the writer wants to be sure people know, but what important fiction. It's like the ideas could walk right of the pages of story and actually be put into real time experience. That's why I wanted to talk with you, thinking we just might share some dreams in common. So I will simply unroll my recent journey ideas.

In my email I told you about going to church with a fellow professor at MIT, Dr. Craig Neilson, and afterwards we went to lunch and talked. I was distraught enough that I wanted to do something, somewhere, which builds a faith that is in considerable contrast to what I heard at church that day. What my friend wanted me to do was to talk to you about what could be done here in my own church. I'm here so infrequently that it's hard to call it my own church, but I like calling it that, especially since the name has been changed to World Citizen Church, and you are here. After I read Dr. Kelly's fourth book again, I got up the courage to do what Dr. Neilson suggested - talk with you."

"My schedule is open all morning," Sandra said without hesitation. "Let me ask my secretary to hold all calls so we can have an open-ended time. In fact, let me call to her office and see if she can bring us some coffee and pastries. You have awakened my interest in what you have been thinking, so I am eager to hear what you have to say."

Dr. Logan began by saying, "Let me recap that morning I went to church with a colleague. He wanted me to attend his church with him. I reluctantly agreed, openly saying that I don't go to church much when I am in Cambridge. To which he replied, 'Neither do I, but it won't do us any harm. It might do us some good, as starchy old professors.' So we went. After church we had lunch together and talked. I assumed he would ask me what I thought of the service. He did just that.

So, while I had a friend I could talk to, who shared some of the same ideas, I unrolled the whole case against a religion so tied to old thinking that current ideas don't even have a chance to get in the door. We talked for an hour. Mostly I talked and he listened. I felt like I was Martin Luther, ready to nail a new thesis to a church door somewhere.

That's when he asked me about my church, how I had said it is different. And, he wanted to know if I had read Dr. James Kelly's book in which the Granddad is speaking at a church that was different. I said that I had read his books, and I wanted to find a church like Center Church where there could be a program ministry like they had there - a church that based their mission in a partnership of science and faith - maybe help that church build a conference center like the one they had.

That's when Dr. Neilson said, "Well, what about your church? You tell me it's different - maybe that's the place you could help create what you are dreaming about."

When I said, "Somebody needs to do something!"

That's when he said, "Welllll?

"Well, what?" I said.

He said, "Well, to repeat, what about your church? Why don't you go talk to your minister about your dreams."

So, here I am sharing with you one of the most outrageous ideas you have ever heard, about creating a conference center like the one at Center Church, in Dr. Kelly's book. So, here I am daring to ask if this kind of model is of any interest to you. But don't answer yet.

Let me go back to the story of my meetings with Craig. He wanted to know what I was thinking or dreaming. He was both sincere and sarcastic. But I said, 'Okay. While I am dreaming, let me dream in terms of my church. So, Dr. Sandra, here's my daring dream.

My dream is that we could have a conference center here at our World Citizen Church like the one at Center Church in Dr. Kelly's book. It would be a place where the Big Ten Universal Qualities are the identity markers we live by and teach. These would define the mission of the center. It would be a place where significant thinkers would come to speak and share their best ideas about how to define and live a great life in our time in history, not somewhere far away, but here in our daily life where we live, here in Alpine and the region beyond. It would be a model for how to be a world citizen right in our own story.

My interest in such a conference center is matched by my being ready to put major financial resources into making the center and its program become real. Somewhere we need to give a "John the Baptist, crying in the wilderness" voice to a faith that links our dreams to the unparalleled potential of this age, so we can build a partnership of science, technology, and faith that reaches across all boundaries of religion, politics, and religion to lead a pioneering new age of enlightenment for our time in history.

There's more detail I could add, but perhaps I have shared enough of my dream to ask if this kind of model is of interest to you. I know it's a bold idea and leading-edge paradigm, so tell me up front if this is of interest you."

Sandra paused and answered out of a sense of awe about such a venture. "Of interest? Yes. I have read enough of Dr. Kelly's books to know that somebody needs to be leading the way forward on creating the kind of new beginnings Dr. Kelly envisions. So, interest, yes, but how could we begin with this kind of venture?"

We could start where I started with such an idea - start with reading Dr. Kelly's books. We could do that here. We could get people to read those books, but especially, *A Place In The Story,* and see what interest that awakens. Would you be willing to do that?"

Dr. Sandra answered thoughtfully as though she were searching. "We could and I may have already begun something in that category. On next Sunday I will begin a series of sermons based in Dr. Kelly's Big Ten Universal Qualities, using one quality for each Sunday. The two could go along together.

But as I have listened to you there is something else that awakens my interest at a level of surprise and wonder. I don't know if I should even connect the two, but let me risk it. I don't know if coincidences are anything more than just that, coincidences. Even so, I am thinking of an unusual coincidence. This past Sunday we had a visitor at our church, who, when he was coming by to shake hands with me at the door, commented about my having quoted from one of Dr. Kelly's books.

I said, 'Dr. Kelly is one of my favorite writers and thinkers.

'He's also one of my favorites,' he said immediately.

'Then you must have read his books.'

'Oh, yes. I not only have read his books, I have heard him tell his stories. I know him. He's my granddad.'

'Really!' I exclaimed. Your granddad! 'No wonder he is your favorite.'

I asked him if he could linger until I could finish speaking to other people so we could talk some more. Then I asked him if he had lunch plans and ventured the idea that we have lunch together, He was open to the idea and we went to the Home at Home restaurant on Main Street. That's when we talked about his being your student guest this summer at your house up on Eagles View Mountain. What do you think? Is this anything more than mere coincidence? Is there any linkage we should wonder about?"

"That is quite a coincidence. I don't usually even know who the students are when they are selected. Dr. Bergstein at the university takes care of that. But in this case I would like to meet this student. Could that be arranged?"

"Yes, of course. But what I am doing is joining that with the idea about reading Dr. Kelly's books in the exploratory stage. Oh, his name is Steve Kelly. What I wonder, Dr. Logan, is if all three of us could read about the conference center in Dr. Kelly's, *A Place In The Story,* and get together soon to talk about what you are proposing."

"That's a great idea, Dr. Sandra. I would like that very much.

Right now all this is in a search-and-dream stage. But I don't want to let it die. Sometimes dreams can be turned into reality, otherwise there's no need to dream. So, let's read together and dream as we read, with a reference to how it might fit with a bold new mission for World Citizen Church."

CHAPTER FIVE

Perspectives from Eagles View

"I liked your sermon this morning.
And I guess I will have to show up regularly
if I am to listen in on the next nine in the series."

STEVE WAS AT CHURCH THE NEXT SUNDAY. AFTER THE SERVICE Sandra spoke with him at the door. "Steve, it's good to see you again," Sandra said. "I didn't know how often you might be attending church, given the need to be at work on your dissertation. I want to talk with you about something."

"Well, I needed a break. Actually, it's more than that. I get some of my best ideas when I am at church or at a concert, or just walking that unique circle on the top of Eagles View Mountain. The mind needs intervals of space and crossover contrasts. That's when the writing mind kicks in and gives you an idea – when you're in the zone. And, as you may well know, that's when you had better write the gist of that idea down before you forget it and can't even recall it. So when I walk the circle on the mountain I always carry pen and paper. Then later, I may find where an idea fits into a backdrop or larger context. But I don't need to tell you that. As someone who has to have a new sermon each week, you are probably well aware of how little bursts of insight become gateway ideas. When you open and enter that little gate it opens up onto a landscape of ideas."

"I understand all that. Totally. It's just as you say," Sandra replied. "Right now I am working on what may be a big gateway idea. So, I have a question. Could we have lunch together? I have something I want to talk with you about."

"That would be great," Steve replied. "Where?"

"Up at your place," Sandra replied immediately with a big smile, and followed with an immediate rejoinder, "Nothing like inviting myself. I have a reason for our meeting at your place. I was hoping we could sit on the deck you have talked about, and overlook the valley below as I open up an idea for your response. If this 'self-invitation' works for you, I want to go by Hearthstone Restaurant and get a take out lunch and bring it up. Unless, of course, you want to cook lunch. Just kidding. I can imagine you like to cook about as much as I, and that's not very much. So, if that works for you, I will need a little time to square things away here. Tell me how to get up there. Then I'll go by and get a carry-out lunch and come on up, if that's okay."

"That's okay with me. But could I go by and get the lunch?"

"You could, of course, but I thought of it first, so I get to be the "cook" in this case. Okay?"

"Well, okay. as you say," Steve yielded. "I'll be waiting for you up on Eagles View."

Steve was waiting when Sandra drove up and walked out the little driveway to meet her. As Sandra opened the door of the car, her immediate response was, "It's cooler up here, maybe ten degrees difference. Thanks for inviting me up, after I invited myself. It's such a delightful place. I have lunch there in the back seat floor, in a box, if you want to get it. Hearthstone does a nice job in carryout dinners. And I am one of their frequent customers."

As they sat on the deck, munching on their sandwiches and looking out into the wonders of the scenery beyond, Steve opened the conversation. "I liked your sermon this morning. And I guess I will have to show up regularly if I am to listen in on the next nine in the series. You said you were going to be focusing on one of the Big Ten Universal Qualities each Sunday. The first one was a really good beginning. And, I liked the way you opened the service. It was so positive and so mind-opening, if that's a good term."

"That is a good term," Sandra said. "I like it. It's what I want to happen. Sometimes the way some services are opened, you are first of all dragged through the mud of negative images – as though that is supposed to make you ever-so-humble – as though the way to respect God is to debase yourself. And I think God may not be at all impressed with this kind of put-down, maybe so tired of it that, in its place, God would want us to announce ourselves at our very best, and without even telling him about it – just thinking it for ourselves. Of course, that assumes that we know that much about God, or what he thinks. Anyway, I like to begin a service with affirmations that announce who we are as part of our reach for our best self."

Steve took a moment to reach back to the table and pick up the bulletin. I read the opening paragraph in the bulletin as I was waiting for you. It fits in this sanctuary up here as well in the sanctuary at the church. It's not about religion, it's about life, about what's sacred. Let me show you what I mean. I know you wrote it, but while you are up here in nature's sanctuary, listen to what you said.

> *With respect for the mystery and oneness of all molecular existence of which we are a part, we have come to reflect on our potential to grow in a faith that honors the collective giftedness we have inherited.*
> *We seek to be accountable to ourselves and to others, as a stewardship of the ages.*

While we are giving our best to life, we will be asking the best of life.
To whatever extent we have failed to reach that quest, we are here to renew that reach, as we learn from all of life.

It's so different from the usual. And I find it interesting how it fits up here where I am writing. How did you come up with this kind of approach?" Steve asked and waited.

"You liked it?" Sandra said in a question that didn't need an answer. "No wonder you liked it. You've known someone who lived with this kind of respect for our humanity and the quest to climb beyond our worst and still continue to reach for our best. I absorbed it from reading your granddad's books. And that's where I got the idea for the sermon series on the Big Ten. And that's what I wanted to talk to you about up here - ideas that have now grown out of your granddad's books in a most unique way."

"But, Sandra," Steve interrupted, "First, I have a question. Why do you end the reading of the scriptures by saying, "The word of God for the people of God?" It may be standard for most churches, but it doesn't fit with your thinking or the church you lead. It may be words about God, but it certainly is not the word of God. There is so much violence, so much narrow self-interest, so many contradictions of reality in the Bible that if one is trying to have integrity, one just cannot say, the word of God. It's just not honest, and to have integrity one must be honest. In fact, honesty is one of the words of the Big Ten. I may be off base, but I tend to think of whatever might be considered to be God's word as something that keeps growing with the progression of knowledge and changing paradigms in successive ages."

"You are right, Steve." Sandra said. "Absolutely right. I guess I just haven't thought that one through before. I get it. I am always ready to learn and I just learned. Thanks, Steve."

Steve was still thinking about the service. He said, "While I am talking about your service, let me compliment you on the affirmation of faith and identity. Like the opening sentences - what is amazing is that those affirmation of faith and identity fit up here just as much as they do in church. And I believe that's as it should be. The old affirmations fit only when you are talking about religion and theology, long-ago-theology. But the affirmations you use are not that way - they are about celebrating life now, and about our plans for our future?

Are you going to use that same affirmation each of the Sundays you talk about the Big Ten?"

"Does that mean you think I should?"

"It does, indeed, especially since you will be talking about the Big Ten qualities of life, not about religion or theology. Let me read the affirmation now, so you can see what I mean about it fitting up here in this world of nature?"

> *I will face this day with confidence.*
> *I have come to this place to search for a new tomorrow, defined by hopes and dreams.*
> *I will live by those dreams which reset my best expectations.*
> *I will make the personal qualities of kindness, caring, honesty, and respect the markers I measure my words and activities by each day.*
> *I will make the relationship qualities of collaboration, tolerance, fairness, and integrity into the ways I live and work with others.*
> *I will make the summit qualities of diplomacy and nobility the peak of my quest to define who I am trying to be in the face of each day's new challenges.*
> *This quest will exceed, and be greater than any of my failures.*

*I will continue to picture myself as I want to be and
announce myself to that goal again and again.
This vision of my journey and quest, will be fulfilled even if they must be part of a long reach
and much renewed effort.*

I was reading the bulletin from church while I was waiting and
especially liked the Affirmation of Faith and Identity. I just wanted
you to know what an uplift the service was and how it blends right
in with this sanctuary up here."

"I certainly can see what you mean by how it fits up here. What
a grand view. In one hundred and eighty degrees all one can see is
cascading mountains and the green of a million trees. Both sanc-
tuaries are places of reflection where we can renew our resolve to
live by the Big Ten which helps us to be that wholesome pleasant
person others want to be around, wherever we are. As I survey
the panoramic view I also see the delightful town of Alpine down
below. That's why I wanted to come up here and sit on this deck.
You had told me how grand the view is. It's everything you said.

The main difference in the traditional Affirmation of Faith and
the one we used at church today is that the traditional affirmation
is about the past and theology - trying to make sure we don't turn
loose of those traditions by repeating and reinforcing them again
and again. This newer affirmation is about making sure we take
hold of the future. It's not protecting what has been so much as
defining what can be. It's about tomorrow and creating vision and
hope. All that figures into why I like being up here so much."

"Oh, that's it," Steve teased. "And I thought it was because you
wanted to sit out here with me."

"Oh, you see through my plot," Sandra teased back, as she
reached over and touched Steve on the hand in a playful gesture.

When she pulled her hand back, Steve reached over and brought
it back and held it. "Okay," he said. "so the secret is out for both
of us. We like this place, but we also like each other, is that it?"

"That's it," Sandra responded as she looked at Steve with a prolonged smile. "And I especially like sharing this time together up here where we look at life from this perspective." Sandra gave his hand a squeeze and then relaxed." They sat in silence, looking out across the view together.

Sandra broke the silence, calling him by name, saying, "Steve, I need your help on thinking about something big. This week professor David Logan, who owns the place up here where you are living this summer, came by to see me. We talked for two hours. I say, "we talked," mostly I listened as he laid out a major proposal. You remember Center Church in Dr. Kelly's book, *A Place In The Story*? That's what he came to talk about. He is proposing that the model that defines the program ministry of Center Church, could become a working model for our church here in Alpine. He is very serious about it and proposes that we create a conference center here like the one at Center Church. He says there are considerable funds from the Vision Foundation, which he heads, that can help make it possible if the church buys into it as an identity and extended mission for the church here in Alpine.

When I indicated an interest and when he learned who you are - that you are Dr. James Kelly's grandson, he could hardly believe the coincidence and liked the idea even more if you could be a part of thinking about this. He said he had no idea that you were Dr. Kelly's grandson, since he is never told anything about the student who gets to live and work up here. As I talked with Dr. Logan, I learned that he and Dr. Kelly have been friends for several years.

As a beginning, Dr. Logan has proposed that the people of the World Citizen Church be invited to read Dr. Kelly's books. Before that happens, he agreed that it would be good if the three of us read *A Place In The* Story and meet to talk. Would you be interested? Maybe there could be some way it would fit into your research thesis of Total Environment. What do you think?"

Steve lingered, in a thinking mood before he answered. "I

had initially planned that I would first immerse myself in Dr. Theodore Gray's book, *The Elements*, as a way of finding out more about where we are in the molecular nature of things, and have already begun that search. But I think I can set that aside for long enough to do what you are asking. It's okay. What I think is that I am being invited to walk in some "mighty tall cotton." So, yes, I would welcome the opportunity. I brought Granddad's books with me, with the intention of working them in at some point. It's his perspective on our humanity that I find so overarching. And that's a term he uses often - overarching. And that's what I get as a by-product from working up here on Eagles View - an overarching perspective on who we are."

Sandra picked up the dialogue. "And that's why I wanted to explore this idea with you up here," Sandra said. "I too am looking for a larger perspective on who we are and are called to be in our time in history, especially as the World Citizen Church."

After discussing Dr. Logan's dream at length, Steve's summation was to confirm their decision. "So the next step for both of us is to read about Granddad speaking at the conference center at Center Church. I will be glad to do that. I look forward to reading about that again. And you will do the same and then we are to meet up here and talk about the next step, is that where we are?"

"That's the plan. It may be easier for you than for me since my duties at the church will go right on," Sandra said as her summation.

Steve and Sandra sat on the deck overlooking the scenery and talking quietly long after they had finished talking about the conference center Dr. Logan was proposing.

Mountain top winds brushed the leaves and chilled the air as they shared journey stories from early years and discovered many parallels. It was like they had known each other a long time and had now just met on a new phase of life's journey of wonder and surprise.

CHAPTER SIX

Entering A New Request of Life

*We want to present our daughter
in a ceremony of baptism soon,
but we have a lot of questions.*

IT WAS MIDMORNING. FROM HER OFFICE WINDOW, SANDRA SAW JIM and Barbara as they came walking up by the side of World Citizen Church. They had called to ask if they could come in and talk. Always so ready to be available to her people, Sandra had said she would be delighted to meet with them.

Barbara was carrying their eight months old daughter and Jim was carrying the "essentials" bag. Sandra went out into the hallway to meet them.

"I am so glad to meet with both of you, and your little girl, whose name is?

"She is Martinette," Jim replied.

Sandra reached out and took her little hand tenderly. "It's so nice to meet you, Martinette. All of you come on in," she said as she led the way.

Sandra led Jim and Barbara and little Martinette over to where they could be seated in a conversational setting. Once all of them were seated, Jim said, "We appreciate your giving us this time to come and talk. We want to present our daughter in a ceremony of baptism soon, but we have a lot of questions. Observations, may be more like it. We were here three weeks ago when our friends presented their baby. We watched every move. Listened to every word. It's the words that are causing us to raise many questions. Frankly, some of the words appear to have come out of Noah's ark. In fact, the ark was mentioned as an instrument of saving people by way of water. But while it was a metaphor, we couldn't help but think of the many people who were not saved in that flood story, as though God didn't care for all people. Why should that be in a baby's baptism? It seems like such a disconnected metaphor.

The words in that old ceremony go on to talk about how God saved the Hebrews as they passed through the waters of the Red Sea. Again, I fail to see a real connection. The infringement on honest, real-time thinking is abysmal.

Maybe you would understand our frustration a little more if you knew that in college, Barbara was a psychology major and I was a philosophy and science major. We don't expect a direct carryover of those paradigms, but we do think they should have some kind of linkage to how we see the world out of our educational perspectives. Take, for instance, in the baptism service the question is asked of the parents, "Do you renounce the spiritual forces of wickedness, reject the evil powers of this world, and repent of your sins?" We don't understand that. What spiritual forces of wickedness, and what evil powers? These concepts come out of the dark ages and should have no place in a service when the parents are committing themselves to surround their child with honorable and wholesome influences in our time in history.

It's so disappointing. There is little reference to how parents can dedicate themselves to building an atmosphere of respect for their baby's world each day. Barbara and I have talked and we think a better ceremony would include a statement in which the parents would say,

On behalf of our child, we affirm our faith in those qualities of life that reward caring and fairness, giving and helpfulness, which honor the teachings and ideals of Jesus. We will seek to be an example of the person we would like to see our baby be and become.

But the ritual used three Sundays ago goes on to say, "Pour out your Holy Spirit, to bless the gift of water and those who receive it, to wash away their sin." What sin? The child is only a baby!"

Dr. Sandra, what made this such a glaring disconnect was when we sat there listening to your sermon Sunday the focus was entirely different. That baptism ceremony was a reference to metaphors from yesterday. But your sermon was a reference to qualities we can adopt to guide us to our best tomorrows. The bulletin listed those qualities and you named them as you began the first of your series of ten sermons on the Big Ten Universal Qualities. Your first sermon on Kindness was great.

When we came home we discussed the ten but focused on three of those qualities we thought applied most to our thoughts about baptism. Care to guess the three we selected?"

"I could," Dr. Sandra said, "but even more I would like to know what you selected."

We focused on kindness, respect, and nobility. We talked about how important kindness is to a baby - how it builds trust and confidence in a baby's emotional development. We talked about respect and noted how much a baby needed to be respected as a real person now, and not just later. We remembered the question children get asked - 'what do you want to be when you grow up?' as though that is the ultimate measure, and childhood is only a preparation for that. It's not. Childhood is real in its own time. And we believe it is important to be respected all along as a fulfilling part of life. Then we talked about nobility and how it is a reference to obligations that grow out of a privileged place in life. As parents of our little girl, we are at a privileged place in life. It is, of course, also a great responsibility, and one we want to fulfill to the best of our ability. And while you were giving your sermon, both of us sat there thinking that the Big Ten Universal Qualities should be a part of a baptism ceremony, and what parents are trying to affirm on behalf of their child. But that concept is not even hinted at in the ceremony we observed a few weeks ago."

With stressful resistance in his voice and manner, Jim said, "Tell me, Dr. Sandra, do we have to use that ceremony? It's an echo of yesterday instead of a vision for tomorrow. We like being a part of this church and we want to present Martinette for baptism, but how can the focus be on a celebration of life, not on some unrelated theology out of the past. Those words do not give us a chance to affirm a great faith we want Martinette to grow up in. Are we required to follow this ceremony? Okay, so I've opened up my feelings, but do we have to use the same ceremony that was used on that Sunday?"

Sandra responded immediately. "I like your understanding of what a baptism should be, with a focus on the Big Ten qualities. Nothing in the standard ceremony begins to match what you have just expressed. So, no, Jim and Barbara, that particular ceremony is not one we would have to use. It's the standard ceremony in our ritual, but I know of nothing that says we have to use it. What do you have in mind?"

"I don't quite know," Jim responded. "We just know that ritual doesn't fit what we are trying to do and say. We want to dedicate ourselves and our little girl to dreams which are a celebration of life here and now that nurture a great faith. What can we do? Do you know of some other ceremonies we can use?"

"Not immediately," Sandra said, slowly. "But I surely do understand your question. I will be glad to search for alternatives."

"Well, could you write one," Jim and Barbara said almost in concert?"

"I have never thought about that, but I certainly will be glad to try," Sandra said, in a searching and pondering manner. "It will be a new venture, but also an opportunity I would welcome. I, myself, have struggled with the references to theology from yesterday, especially that reference to sins being washed away. I am no more pleased with the ritual than you. Maybe we could work together on one. Would you be willing to write down some of the ideas you have just expressed. And I will create a draft of some of mine and then, we could meet again next week to put our ideas together. Would that be something you would like to do?"

Jim looked over at Barbara and noted her positive expression. "That would be excellent," Jim said. Immediately Barbara added her comment. "That would be wonderful. It would be a privilege for us to work with you on that."

When they met a week later, Sandra led the way down the hall to the nursery. "I think this may be our best place for all of us." Jim put Martinette down on the carpet and Barbara brought some toys over for her to play with. They watched her use her little fingers to pick up items while they all sat around on the floor and edited the new ceremony. After they had deleted some words and added others they soon had a whole new ceremony. When it was complete, Jim said, "I am so pleased. This helps us to say what we want to say on behalf of Martinette and the future we want to share with her as she grows in her own faith, and as we grow in ours.

On the next Sunday morning Dr. Sandra announced the service of baptism with a new sense of excitement. She paused as she looked down at Jim and Barbara, who were waiting to present Martinette in sacred moments of dedication. She said, "Before I invite Jim and Barbara to come forward to present their daughter, Martinette, for baptism, I want to explain the reason this baptismal ceremony is different from usual. One very special reason is that Jim and Barbara helped to write it. And, Martinette helped, too, as she sat on the floor and played while we put words of hope and dreams together on her behalf, to announce a faith that celebrates the Big Ten Universal Qualities. You should have heard Jim talk about how he thought baptism should be a celebration of life in the present moment for children, not just as though it is some kind of extension of theology or initiation ceremony. Jim and Barbara said they believe a service of baptism should reference the future, not the traditions of the past – that it should reference a very special time in the life of loving parents to affirm a partnership of parent and child that expresses a living faith. I liked the focus he expressed when he said, the focus should not be on something done for a baby so much as something parents can do to build a dream in progress, and as a journey of faith together. So Jim, Barbara, and I worked together to make this a very special moment to celebrate dreams and quality of life now.

In this service, when the reference is to the old prophet, Simeon, it is a backdrop on an earlier time, when the parents of Jesus took their little baby to their temple for a dedication which parallels a service of baptism in our time. It was there that the beloved prophet turned his attention to Jesus, held him in his arms, and announced his vision dream for Jesus. That's the proper focus for a service of baptism in which loving parents make promises as a guiding sacred influence and journey of faith.

That's the kind of faith Jim and Barbara want to announce as they pledge their sacred support for Martinette's growing faith.

So I now reverently invite Jim and Barbara to present their daughter, Martinette, for baptism, accompanied by the support of loving family and friends.

When Jesus was just beginning his teaching ministry he left his home in Nazareth and walked many miles to where John the Baptist was preaching on the banks of the Jordan River. When people were coming down to the river to be baptized by John as their commitment to his dreams for the future, Jesus was among them and was baptized by John.

It was a turning point for Jesus and a way of announcing himself as a leader of a dream of a kingdom of heaven on earth. Later, when Jesus was in that same area, just east of the Jordan River, great crowds came to listen to Jesus as he taught them.

Some mothers were bringing their children to Jesus and he blessed them. When the disciples were telling them not to bother Jesus he said, "Let the children come to me! Never send them away!"

The importance of that kind of respect for children was already being expressed when Jesus was only eight days old and his parents took him to the temple for a service of dedication. An old prophet named, Simeon, was at the temple that day and saw Joseph and Mary carrying Jesus across the Temple courtyard. He walked over slowly and greeted them. When he looked at Jesus, he saw the promise of the future. He asked if he could hold Jesus. He took Jesus in his arms and said a prayer of thanksgiving and hope. In Jesus, he saw the new beginnings of a vision for the future he had longed for across many years.

Today young parents have brought their child to a temple of reverence in their time and place in the human story. They seek to honor the qualities Jesus lived out in his story. Those qualities have come into new focus in our time as the Big Ten Universal

Qualities. These qualities can be affirmed by any person, anywhere in the world family as the identity markers they choose to live by in their own story.

These foundational guiding words include the personal qualities of Kindness and Caring, Honesty, and Respect. They embrace the self-chosen relationship markers of Collaboration and Tolerance, Fairness, and Integrity. They reach a summit in the qualities of Diplomacy, and Nobility. When these qualities are input into the mind of a young child as a faith to live by, and modeled by parents, that circular feedback becomes a guiding and renewing atmosphere for honoring the teachings and model set by Jesus.

Jim and Barbara have chosen these qualities to affirm their faith and aspirations as they present their child for baptism.

_____*Jim*_____ and ___*Barbara*___, as parents, do you affirm that these are the qualities you seek to live by in your own life as you nurture and guide the life of your child?

They are.

Even as Simeon received Jesus into his arms and blessed him, I now receive ___*Martinette*___ into my arms at this temple of faith.

(Minister receives child)

    Martinette , you are richly blessed to have parents whose vision for your future is based in ten universal qualities, especially kindness, respect, and nobility. Even as it was said of Jesus that he increased in 'wisdom and stature before God and man,' may you grow and learn to honor those guiding qualities your parents now envision for you. These will lead you to enter your own request of life day by day and year by year at its highest level.

(Minister places water on forehead and says)

    Martinette , I baptize you in the name of Jesus. May the faith your parents have af-firmed on your behalf become a faith you live by as you give your best to life as your request of life.

Let us all pray together.

God of the lengthening human story, as with the prophet, Simeon, at a temple of faith, we also see the promise of the future. Our prayer is that this child, and all of us, may fulfill a place in the story where we live out those qualities modeled in the life of Jesus and his dream of a kingdom of heaven on earth. Amen.

It was a tender and cherished sacred moment as Dr. Sandra re-turned Marionette into the arms of loving parents who had entered a special request of life at their temple of faith.

CHAPTER SEVEN

Dreams Becoming Real

"The time has come to turn dreams into reality. We must begin."

EXCITEMENT WAS GROWING AS STEVE, SANDRA, AND DR. LOGAN MET on the Look Beyond deck up on Eagles View Mountain to explore the possibility of creating a conference center modeled on the one described in *A Place In The Story*. Instead of diminishing their dreams, the reading they had done, had increased their sense of the need for such a conference center and the confidence they could help make it a reality.

The first thing they decided was that such a center would bear the name, World Citizen Center, as a connection with the World Citizen Church, but not be directly linked to the church. The link would be that the minister of the World Citizen Church, the chair of the Council, and its chair of Education would be standing members of the World Citizen Center Board of Directors. When it was suggested that Dr. Logan be on the board, he respectfully declined, choosing only to be advisory to the board. But what he said gave a green light to their dreams. He said, "The Vision Foundation I have created will invest significantly in such a center, both in its launch and building phase, and its ongoing programs."

When Steve and Sandra spoke of his generosity, Dr Logan reminded them that it would be an extended stewardship of the gifts that had been entrusted to his care by his parents, and their parents before them. Explaining more he said, "The Vision Foundation funds have grown to the point that it has become an accumulation of resources in search of a place to build dreams. The time has come to turn dreams into reality. We must begin. With your help we can dare to begin turning dreams into plans.

I have been told that it's good to visualize your dreams. Ever since our last meeting I have been doing just that. I can see the World Citizen Center in my mind now. It will be somewhere near the church. It will be a magnificent structure that inspires vision for the future. It will give the Big Ten Universal Qualities visibility. It will be a voice that defines the better people anyone can be as a world citizen in the greatest time for shaping the future that the world has ever known.

My dreams include your giving me the go-ahead-courage to engage an architect who will draw up a prospectus of the World Citizen Center. I can see it already. Let share my vision that I will describe to an architect.

It must be on an elevated area with a rather large footprint. It will occupy the crest of the hill with an outside appearance that will stand as a monument to humanity's dream and reach for a great future. It will be simple and basic in design, but reflect elegance and majesty. The architect will design a large contemporary abstract design to symbolize the boldness of the world citizen identity. I envision that icon as a towering abstract structure resembling the logo that Dr Kelly has at the beginning of each chapter in his books. These three triangles and towering three gleaming white pylons will stand slightly higher than the building itself and be just to the left of the main entrance.

From a front view, one will see a long building with tall glass walls, interspersed with marble fluted square half columns, or pilasters. Just in front of that will be a patio as long as the building, with a wrought iron banister running along the edge. That will be just above a steep slope of shrubbery, extending down the slope to the parking area.

Inside, a long sky-lighted atrium will run parallel to the outside patio. Spaced in that long blue carpeted area, there will tables and lounge chairs to create an informal socialization area like that of the lobby of major hotel. This social area will be just in front of a large banquet hall, which can be sectioned off like those of major convention centers. Supporting this well be a state of the art kitchen and service area. The center will have four conference rooms, lots of restrooms, four offices - everything first class, but simple in design and without being ostentatious.

I envision one of those conference rooms being a place to dream bold dreams like, we have done up here on Eagles View Mountain. It will be on the front corner, next to the abstract icon just outside, with a floor-to-ceiling glass wall that gives one a view of Eagles View Mountain. That conference room will overlook a garden area with low growing shrubbery. From there one can look up and see Eagles View Mountain, where future leaders can do what we are doing up here now - dreaming dreams that can help make the world better. In fact, that's what I see as the purpose of the whole World Citizen Center - a place to dream our best dreams for a greater future for the human family that lives by the Big Ten Universal Qualities!

As I sit here overlooking Alpine, in my dream I already see the World Citizen Center. It will be a new launch pad for humanity's unparalleled lengthening future of new beginnings beyond successive old endings.

But, right now, let's pick up on the plan to get the people on board with the dream. It's the place where you, Sandra, can be a pivotal person in all we are talking about - the one who can bring the people of World Citizen Church into the dream and its noble reach for new tomorrows.

So, I believe we are ready to go with the phase in which Sandra leads the people of the World Citizen Church in reading Dr. Kelly's books, especially, *A Place In The Story* After that we can have an initiating, open meeting of the Church Council where we set forth both a verbal and visual plan for a World Citizen Center as a place to build a better world family.

After Sandra leads the way in getting the people of the church on board, we can rely on Steve to be the person who leads the launch and creation of the World Citizen Center! It's all part of my dream.

Dr. Logan's summation was interrupted by Lester Sawyer tapping on the glass sliding door. Steve got up and opened the door. Quietly, Lester said, "I am sorry to interrupt your planning, but Carlena and I have your refreshments ready. Could we bring them out here now?"

"Yes. Please," Steve said. "Your timing is perfect. And thank you so very much. Ever since I came here you have been so very helpful and this is just one more way you have been so gracious."

We are at a point when it's time to celebrate!

As they shared in the refreshments, Sandra went over and stood at the handrail overlooking Alpine. "Come and look," she invited. "See the steeple of World Citizen Church from here. Look just beyond that. There, at the upper edge of the parking lot, is a tract of land that belongs to the church because a few years earlier, one of the church members said, 'I won't be here much longer. If the church will accept it, I want to give the land that adjoins the church parking lot for future expansion.'

Turning to Dr. Logan and directing a question to him, she said, "Dr. Logan, can you envision the World Citizen Center there?"

"I can, indeed!" Dr. Logan said with a sense of awe. "If that becomes the place for our dreams, we must be ready to take our dreams to the place!

But what I see by looking at my watch is that I have a plane to catch to get back to MIT. So I must head back down the mountain now and leave the plan in your hands. I leave with great confidence about the future of the World Citizen Center."

As Dr. Logan shook hands with Steve and Sandra just before leaving for the airport he said, "It has been rightly said that money follows great ideas. I believe we are engaged in a great idea. Count me in! And count the Vision Foundation in on a dream worthy of its capital resources. It's a time to give our dreams a chance to happen!"

CHAPTER EIGHT

Dreams in Motion

*That is our guiding goal - doing what we can
to make a better world by being better people!*

GETTING THE PEOPLE OF WORLD CITIZEN CHURCH TO READ DR.
Kelly's books, mainly *A Place In The Story,* and getting a select
group of fifteen to serve as an Exploratory Committee was easy.
Interest was immediate. As a way to build a larger base for understanding the plan for a World Citizen Center, anyone who was
interested was given the opportunity to read Dr. James Kelly's
books. To support that open invitation, Dr. Logan said that his
Vision Foundation would make all of Dr. Kelly's books available
without charge to anyone in the church who would read any one,
or all of them.

When the Exploratory Committee and the Church Council
met, it was an open meeting. Any member could attend to hear
about plans for the World Citizen Center. The Fellowship Hall of
the World Citizen Church was filled. Chairs were set in a large
semi-circle so everyone could feel included.

Dr. Logan flew back in from MIT to be a part of the meeting

and eagerly awaited Dr. Sandra's introduction so he could make the proposal to create the World Citizen Center.

When Dr. Sandra addressed the meeting, she was aware of the history making nature of their meeting. She began quietly. "We believe we are engaged in being disciples of Jesus on mission in a new age. One of today's extended disciples of Jesus in our time, has a bold new idea worthy of our open exploration.

One day Dr. James Logan came to my office, distressed that the church was not keeping up with the progressive advances in the human story in our age of marvel and newness – that important religious ideas were so locked in the past that they were out of sync with the progression of knowledge. That's when he ventured the dream that the conference center described in the book, *A Place In The Story,* could be reproduced here in Alpine. We all have been reading about it that for the past few weeks. To tell you about this I want to ask Dr. David Logan to share his dream."

Dr. Logan was seated in the semi-circle of chairs. He stood and walked over to the edge of the circle where a perspective drawing of the proposed World Citizen Center was on an easel, still draped with a light blue cloth. Dr. Logan spoke quietly, but with excitement. "Thank you Dr. Sandra. And thank you fellow members, for the opportunity to share a dream with you that I hope we can make become real.

A local architect has been engaged to draw up a prospectus of what the structure of a World Citizen Center here in Alpine might look like. We are pleased to have the opportunity to share it with you now." Dr. Logan reached over and slowly pulled the cloth off and laid it on a nearby table. "What I have just uncovered is the physical part of a dream that can come alive and be a fulfilled here in Alpine. But the shape and design of that building is not nearly as important as the dream that the conference center we are proposing can help us fulfill the vision expressed in one of the hymns we sing with these defining words:

To serve the present age,
My calling to fulfill;
O may it all my powers engage
To do my master's will.

We are here as dreamers who are seeking to create a World
Citizen Center to expand the teaching ministry of our church by
doing what we can to build a better world by being better people.

We can begin to build our dream together under the leadership
of a very special person who has come to Alpine to live up in my
place on Eagles View. His name is Steve Kelly. He is working on
his PhD in environmental science.

Kelly is a name we all have heard before. You've read books
by a person named Kelly. You can imagine my surprise when Dr.
Sandra said, 'Steve Kelly is the grandson of Dr. James Kelly, whose
philosophy you have read about in his most unusual books. I had
read Dr. Kelly's books before, but I have read them again now,
along with you.

Those books changed the way I see the world and my place in
the story. Out of that new, open ended paradigm of the way things
can be, I came to visit Dr. Sandra and shared a dream I had that
conference center like the one described in the book, *A Place In
The Story,* could be reproduced here.

To explore that dream, Dr. Sandra, Steve, and I sat on the
deck of my little "Look Beyond" Cottage up on Eagles View and
dreamed together. That has now resulted in a visual presentation
that our architect has now put together in a beautiful prospectus.
We have asked Steve Kelly to lead us in the creation of the World
Citizen Center, once it is approved. But Steve has also been asked
to assume an even more important responsibility. We are asking
Steve to make sure we keep connected to the vision and faith his
granddad has put into his books about a knowledge-based faith and
the identity markers of the Big Ten Universal Qualities. We need
his young, creative mind to keep us true to our dreams.

One of the words in the Big Ten is integrity. For all we are proposing, to have integrity, we must first do our own personal best to live out these qualities, and then make them central in what we do as the World Citizen Center. There is nothing to be marketed or sold, just a big, demanding set of qualities to be lived and shared. We believe anyone who tries to make these qualities real in his or her own story will be a more successful person and a world citizen. That is our guiding goal. It's doing what we can to make a better world by being better people!

The goal is to help us live out world citizen qualities right here in Alpine. The goal is to keep us informed by bringing some of the best speakers from all a cross our country to the World Citizen Center to help us build a partnership of a knowledge-based faith with science and technology.

I know this is a big dream. But it is part of a big dream this church has already represented by choosing to put an icon of the Master Teacher on the altar of this church.

I believe the teachings of Jesus have been represented anew and refocused in the Big Ten Universal Qualities. When we choose the Big Ten as our identity markers, we will have created an umbrella under which we will be far more ready to do the right thing as new situations arise wherever we have opportunities to develop the "better angels of our nature."

While our dream plans for a World Citizen Center have been progressing here, another dream has been progressing. I have been asked to become a full time professor of International Studies and Social Policy at MIT. I have accepted that position, but that in no way detours my deep interest in creating this overarching dream we can build together here. I will shuttle in and out whenever I am needed. The big plus is that you will be more involved in the dream. Dr. Sandra and Steve will bring together a team of people more capable than I to advance the plans that make the World Citizen Center become a real place in time.

All of us, whatever our respective place in the story here in

Alpine, can be a part of an important new story. We can create a World Citizen Center to extend the kingdom of heaven dream, as Alpine's place in the story, and our place in the story to honor the proverb of Solomon, who said, *"The intelligent man is always open to new ideas. In fact, he looks for them."*

So many of you have now read some or all of Dr. Kelly's books. Together we can extend the world citizen identity he defined. We believe we are engaged in building a place where great ideas can be expressed again and again. All the while, you will have my full support and the financial support of the Vision Foundation.

I believe this is a dream whose time has come."

As Dr. Logan took his seat, there was a brief respectful and thoughtful silence, which was followed by an hour-long give and take discussion. Any person was free to speak.

Deep into the discussion, Bronson Holbrook spoke quietly and intently. "What I have read in the books and hear people talking about is how we can be a world citizen without ever leaving our day to day location. I see the potential of the World Citizen Center to help us do that. I believe we can go forward with the dream."

Reginald Palmer followed that statement of faith, and said, "I say let's go with the whole idea." He was usually quiet in such meetings, but when he spoke, people listened with a high level of respect and trust. He continued. "Reading these books, speak for me far beyond anything else I have ever read. They say something which needs to be said in our time, and something I have wished many times I could hear someone say. I like what Dr. Kelly says about the future, and that we must listen for a call from the future in order to fill a place in our present story that honors the mind, respects our collective knowledge, and gives purpose and guidance to the new tools we are creating day by day that add to our poten-tial to build our greatest tomorrows. It's what I have been hungry for a long time. I am ready to support it all the way with what I can give, in full confidence that we can make this a major extension of the World Citizen Church's ministry. It's our time to take a giant step forward. So, I say let's go with it."

It was Wilma Atkins who started the applause. After the second clap of her seventy-seven year old hands, others joined quickly until almost everyone was a part of it.

Then came an immediate contrasting quietness when Oscar Mayes cut in quickly and said emphatically, "This will split our church. We are not ready for this. We can never do it. It's grandiose and out of step with what the church is supposed to be doing. We are supposed to be preaching the gospel and teaching the truth of the Bible, not spreading the latest ideas of science and the modern learning that comes with it. Count me out. And you can count a lot of other people out too. I can't believe what is happening to the church in our time. It's not being true to the Bible. We need more time to think about it before we take on such a big move, such a risky departure from who we have been."

The atmosphere was suspenseful. Quiet. Sandra wondered if it were her time to say something, but waited. She knew it was time for the people to speak.

Reginald Palmer stood up again. Even more slowly than he had spoken before he said, "I know it's a big change." He turned to Oscar and said. "Oscar, you have one of the most up-to-date business ventures in this whole area. I respect your sense of caution and desire to make right decisions. We all know you and respect what you think. But I believe when you think about this some more and see its real possibilities, you will become one of its biggest supporters. I just know you that well. We all do. In the long run I am sure we can count on you. You are just that kind of person. And if anyone leaves the church you won't be one of them." Reginald remained standing as Oscar responded.

Quietly, slowly, and thoughtfully, Oscar said, "Yes, you are right, Reginald. I spoke to quickly. I will never leave this church. It's been a part of my family and my life for all these years. And so

I will go ahead and speak only for myself and say, if this becomes the majority opinion of the church, I assure you that I will come around from what I said and be right in there pitching."

Reginald was still standing and spoke again. "The people of this church are like you, Oscar. We stand together. And we all know that the best success stories are written, not when everything is easy and there is no challenge, but the real success stories are written against a backdrop of challenges big enough to awaken our best effort. That's also when motivation grows equal to the challenge. That's why this church has so much credibility in this town. Some say this church has always been a leader of tomorrow. So, yes, this is a big challenge, but because it is just that, it has an even better chance of success. And because we are among the most progressive thinkers in Alpine, I know the identity set forth in Dr. Kelly's books will continue to inspire us and cause us to think of ourselves as world class citizens. It's time for us to dream those dreams which are big enough to signal us for the next level up."

An immediate applause ended his speech. Everyone knew that with both Oscar and Reginald supporting the venture, and with this kind of, "I can" attitude the program had a good chance of being a major success.

"So, Dr. Sandra," Reginald said as he turned to her, "lead us to the next step forward. What do we need to do?"

Dr. Sandra responded in a professional manner, but still in her usual and cordial way. "The next step forward is not a lot different from most major new ventures for a church. We will need the Church Council to create a Board of Directors, then a Building Committee, which will get Dr. Logan's architect to develop working drawings for the prospectus he has already created. And if there is any kind of loan involved, it will have to be presented to the full membership.

In the process of talking about our ideas, some have said, 'Why can't we begin the program now, using our present fellowship hall as a temporary home of the World Citizen Center? Of course we can discuss that. But we would have to ask ourselves if that would take the steam out of our full plans and the incentive and momentum we already have going under Dr. Logan's leadership."

Dr. Logan walked back up and stood beside the prospectus and spoke again, quietly. He said, "If you can move ahead with the plan offered here there will be no loan. I will commit my Vision Foundation to give the kind of support needed to make the World Citizen Center into a vital extension of the ministry of our church. My hope is that we can move ahead immediately. This a time for us to invest in a new tomorrow for a new era oneness in the human story."

The philosopher, Lao-Tzu, said 'A journey of a thousand miles must begin with a single step.' This is a time to take that single step."

CHAPTER NINE

Uncertainty on the Yellow Brick Road

*"What I want to say first is that I appreciate
your coming in to talk with me."*

"DR. SANDRA," OSCAR MAYES SAID, AS SOON AS HE WAS INVITED
into her office and sat down across the desk for her, "I owe it to
you and the church to tell you what's happening here. And I don't
like what's happening. It's not fair to you, or me, or the church.
But, there's a group in the church that is against the conference
center and the speakers program - a group that objects to it being
a part of our church, and they are working behind the scenes to
block it by getting you moved from here. Sometimes the minister
is the last person to know when things like this are happening. So
I have come out of a sense of responsibility to give you this update.

These people are quietly going about their scheme. They have
formed an ad hoc committee and have gone to see the district
superintendent. I know, that's not how it's supposed to happen,
that only the duty elected committee is supposed to do this, but
the district superintendent has received them anyway, and you can

tell by the tone of my voice that I don't like that. Word is that he received them under the pretense that they were concerned about the church budget and wanted to talk to him about that. But, of course, that's not how it is. I am involved in the finances of the church enough to know the budget is in good shape. And even if it were not, there are enough resources here to make it in good shape any time we are asked to pitch in and help. Some of these people are withholding their giving and using that to support their resistance, even bragging about it. But in spite of all that, the budget is fine. Some others may even be giving more. What I know the budget is fine. Already our new venture is attracting new members who may be giving gladly. Anyway, what the ad hoc committee is really trying to do is to block the World Citizen Center by getting you moved. And I don't like that. Don't like it at all. The more I realized what's happening the more I knew I had to come and talk to you.

So thank you for letting me come in. What is also involved is that I am getting dragged into all this as though I am in favor of the opposition, and that's not how it is. I think you need to know that. They are using my name and what I said at that initial meeting. They say that I said a lot of people would leave the church, without adding the rest of what I also said. I know, I did indicate that I would leave, but that's not how I left it. I assured them that if people left World Citizen Church I certainly wouldn't be one of them. What I assured them was that I would go along with the majority. But they don't talk about that latter part. They keep twisting it. They don't care whether it's true or not. The more they repeat their twisted story, the more they believe it. They just keep using it to support their bias.

So, Dr. Sandra, after loosing sleep over this for too many nights, I decided that I had to come and talk to you and let you know personally how I stand on all this. I am not a part of their plot and not about to leave the church. In fact, I have become very interested in this new way of seeing who we can be as a leading-edge church. So, Dr. Sandra, what do you know about all this?" He breathed a sigh after completing his long explanation and waited for her response.

"Well, Oscar," Sandra answered slowly. "What I want to say first is that I appreciate your coming in to talk with me. It's good to know where you stand. I already had the feeling that you were not a part of this. I heard it by the grapevine. So, I already knew.

I am aware of much of what is going on. Not all, but a lot of it. And I am aware that the district superintendent met with the ad hoc committee. But after that, he met quietly with the church's duly authorized committee. That was after he had talked with the bishop, who, as I hear it, really made the district superintendent stand in the corner for receiving that ad hoc committee - said pointedly that he was never to receive any committee but the standing church committee to speak for the church.

Out of all this, I had a call from the bishop's office, updating me on all that was taking place and asking Dr. Logan and me to meet with him and the district superintendent in his office. And that's where it stands now.

So, Mr. Mayes, as goes political unrest and spin, we may not have heard the last from this group. But Dr. Logan and I will go and listen to what the bishop has go say. While we share the usual anxiety when things are unsettled, we will keep telling ourselves to see how we can turn all this into some kind of opportunity. So stay positive. I will update Steve on what's happening after we get back from our meeting with the bishop. Then, at some point, I will call you to fill you in."

CHAPTER TEN

In the Bishop's Office

"It's about shaping the future and making history as we go."

"HELLO, STEVE," SANDRA SAID ON THE PHONE. "DR. LOGAN AND I were called to the "principal's office" and I wonder if we could meet so I could fill you in on that meeting that took place yesterday morning?"

"Of course," Steve said immediately, responding to the sense of importance in Sandra's voice. "Should I come down the mountain, or would you like to come up here?"

"Up there, if it's all right. I can stop by and get some lunch and bring it up. Would an hour from now be okay?"

"That would be fine. I will be interested in your report. See you soon."

As he had done each time Sandra came up to Eagles View, Steve went out to meet her at her SUV. "You sounded urgent. Is everything okay?" Steve asked.

"Yes. At least I think so. I'll tell you about it when we get inside. It's chilly up here today. I hope you have a fire in the fireplace."

"Oh, yes." Steve said as he picked up the carryout lunch and said,

"Come on in where it's warm. Mr. Sawyer keeps plenty of wood right by the entrance door and I have had a fire on several of the cool mornings. Sitting by the warm fireplace is just one of the things I love about being up here, especially when we can share it together."

With their lunch placed on the table, they both backed up to the fireplace and took a moment to get warm before they sat down across from each other. Sandra opened up the lunch boxes and took out their sandwiches. "Guess I left you a little anxious when I called. I shouldn't have. Everything still seems to be set on, go. So, let me tell you about our meeting as near like it happened as I can, verbatim style.

When Dr. Logan and I arrived at the bishop's office we were invited in immediately and cordially received by Bishop Watson. The district superintendent, Marsden Short, was there and obviously they had already been talking about the situation before we arrived.

After a few moments of cordial conversation, Bishop Watson said, 'The full cabinet of district superintendents is already in session down in the conference room, dealing with a few other things, but I thought it would be good for them to hear your story. So, let's walk down the hall and cut in on their meeting.' He teased and said, 'I don't know why they would let me cut in like that, but for some reason a bishop gets to do that.'

When Bishop Watson asked us to tell our story, I deferred to Dr. Logan, and with that he began to tell about his dream for the World Citizen Center with his usual excitement about it.

Early in his presentation he stopped abruptly and said, 'If you would like to get a fuller understanding of what all this about you can read it in four books by Dr. James Kelly. And just in case there are some of you who have never read these books, and don't know much about me, I can tell you that I am one of Dr. Kelly's book peddlers. I've done it a lot. I've given away dozens of his books. And I would be pleased to send copies of all of his books to any of you who have not read them.'

Dropping into a television commercial mode, he mimicked and said, 'You can get these amazing books for only nineteen-ninety-five each. And I can send them to you free of shipping and handling during this special offer, if you call in the next ten minutes.'

Extending the play on TV commercials in a teasing parallel, he added, 'But, as a one time offer for this assembled group, I will send them to you on a thirty day trial offer. And if you are not absolutely convinced these are some of the most positive leading-edge books you have ever read, you can . . . you can just keep them and, well… read them again.'

When Dr. Logan finished his satirical tease he said, 'I will be glad to peddle Dr. Kelly's books to any of you. Just hand me your business card and you will receive these books in the mail. First, you have to go ahead and hand me your card.'

He smiled as soon as they began to pass in their cards, and continued with his excited description of World Citizen Church and the plans for a related World Citizen Center. They listened with intense interest as he told about his dream of a center that would make the Big Ten Universal Qualities into a major new paradigm for a greater future.

"Steve, you know already that I like to do verbatims, so let me continue telling what Dr. Logan said."

"I know that," Steve cut in. "And you're good at it. Please proceed."

Sandra continued. "Dr. Logan said, 'I am just standing by in amazement about what we are doing. I believe that when our church decided to change the name to World Citizen Church, the mission of the church changed. It's as though we were passing from being just a parochial and rather standard church, into being a church ready to redefine our mission with a world family identity. It's not so much looking back on who we have been, as looking forward to who we can be. It's about shaping the future and making history as we go.'

Dropping out of his promotion tone of voice, Dr. Logan said

in a more serious and personal tone, 'I think of Martin Luther and his nailing his Ninety-five Thesis to the church door. The thesis I would like to nail to the church door, and the worship places of the world as an overarching template for identity is, the commanding vision set by the Big Ten Universal Qualities. These ten defining qualities move the markers on the field and measure by the oneness of the whole human family grid and by how well we are doing by being, just good people, not by which culture, or politics, or religion is best, but by how good we are as a world family. The more people who link the Big Ten qualities with the amazing progression of our science and technology, the closer we get to a winning touchdown that scores a big win for all the world. Nobody looses. Everybody wins!'"

Sandra was still caught up in the positive emotions of Dr. Logan's speech and its self energizing feedback loop, and said, "Steve, I wish you could have been there and heard him in person." Anyway, when Dr. Logan dropped back into a quieter mode he said, 'It may seem like an oversimplification, but this is something that works. The more people who make these ten words their own personal self-chosen identity base, the greater the potential for achieving a higher humanity and resulting better civil society.'"

Sandra took a breath and continued her verbatim of Dr. Logan's speech. 'The Big Ten qualities are self-rewarding. And why wouldn't they be? When we live by the personal qualities of kindness, caring, honesty, and respect, and the relationship words of collaboration, tolerance, fairness, and integrity, and the summit words of diplomacy and nobility, we become more confident and become winners! And, if you might even think this is easy, all you have to do to find out otherwise, is simply to pick one of these words as your One-A-Day identity marker, then measure yourself by that quality all day long in every situation. And, like me, you may find yourself getting up again with stumped toes and skinned knees. In the long run these words can write themselves into your identity in such a way that they are not just directives, but correctives - real-time checks and balances. That's when you have the opportunity to get up, bush the dust off and try again and again until you turn old endings into new beginnings.'

When Dr. Kelly talked about this, he said, 'This concept is at the heart of what is best in the Bible, especially the *Proverbs of Solomon*. The Big Ten qualities define the future's best options. They inform the brain to lead the way. These chosen qualities become an inner Identity GPS. And the world needs this kind of positive GPS as never before!'

Dr. Logan was animated. He paused a moment, then looked around slightly and said, 'This is a unique moment. Here I am, a scientist, preaching to the preachers. But, of course, that's as it ought to be, with both of us preaching to each other. Our faith needs to be informed by other perspectives besides sacred texts. Our faith needs to be about helping people live the good life in a complex world, not just how to be religious.'

I watched as Dr. Logan sat on the edge of his seat and said, 'The emerging mission of the World Citizen Center is to help people use their gifts and skills here and now to live by a world citizen identity right where they live, on location, as their own unique place in the story. One's own place in today's collective human story is a place to shape the future by a sunrise paradigm right where we live. We don't need to go somewhere else. This place is fine. It's a time for us. It's a place for us. It's a time to achieve a more noble identity. This is the time to help humanity rise to its next level up, one example at a time. This is the time to be on stage and to energize one's own story with a very rewarding feedback loop.

So the World Citizen Center is to be a conference center where we will bring in the world's leading-edge speakers who can give a voice to this dream and vision. These chosen speakers can give guidance for making our best informed decisions.

Just as we have break-thru technologies we need church identity break-thru so we align with the new paradigms of how to see the world and its future.

Our best history writes forward, not backwards, and writes faster than ever before. We have tremendous increasing potential to write our story in terms of the future we ask for.

The big, long-term goal is for anyone, anywhere in the world to come to a place in their story where they could be asked, "Do you know about The Big Ten Universal Qualities?" and they would answer, "Yes! I am trying to be one of the world's wholesome, pleasant, fun-to-be-around persons - a Big Ten world citizen.'

Dr. Logan eased back in his chair and said, 'I probably already having taken more time than you could spare, but I wanted you to know what the World Citizen Center is all about, not just as a place, but as an ideology - a dream for our world family. The energizing assumption is that this is an opportune time to adopt a new knowledge-based faith that overarches politics, culture, and religion to define a template of identity based in the oneness of all existence and our potential as the human family to make this the greatest age the world has ever known! Without this kind of mission to humanity, the church surrenders its credentials as a leader of the future. But if we get the learning centers of the world to teach these Big Ten Universal Qualities and choose them for their daily identity markers, these word tools will change the future and we all will be winners!'"

Sandra paused from her excited verbatim and said, "Listen at me. I sound just like he sounded that day.

Anyway, to continue, Bishop Watson waited a thoughtful moment before he responded and said, 'That's the best sermon I have heard in a long time! I wish all of our churches could hear a sermon like that. It's a sermon all of us should be giving. What I fear more than losing members because of this kind of preaching, is losing our integrity if we don't do this kind of preaching - if we fail to move forward with a faith that matches our growing science and technology.'

Bishop Watson turned to Dr. Logan and said, 'Thank you for

this new version of a ninety-five thesis to nail to the church door. Keep your hammer handy. I need you. All of us here need you. The church needs you!'

Sandra paused a moment in her energized recap of Dr. Logan's presentation and said, "I remember what Dr. Logan said when we came back to the car. He said, 'That was fun. That's the first time I ever got to preach to preachers. And it didn't feel bad at all. In fact, it felt good, like that is the way it should be - a two-way sermon.'"

Steve looked at Sandra and said, "Wow. You had me concerned when you called, but it turns out that what you had was a great report. So, how does that old song go? "If I had a hammer, I'd hammer out ..."

When Sandra got back down the mountain she went to her office where the first thing she did was to call Oscar Mayes and tell him about their meeting with Bishop Watson.

When she finished, Mr. Mayes said, "What a relief. I was beginning to loose sleep over this until I finally decided I had to talk with you. I'm glad I did. I am sorry you are having to go through all this opposition here. I know you always stay in the positive zone, but I didn't realize what a positive direction all this was taking. I'm no poet, but I do remember a poem by Frank L Stanton, and his recurring phrase, "keep a-goin!" More than ever you have my full backing and we just need to 'keep a-goin'! So, thanks for giving me this call. I am feeling better already. With that kind of positive response from the bishop, you won't be moving from here. I am very glad. Now I probably won't be able to sleep from being so excited!"

Oscar had a tone of gratitude in his voice as he closed the phone call. With great respect he said, "Thanks, Dr. Sandra."

In response, Sandra said, "And thank you, Mr. Mayes. I know it took some honest courage for you to open up on all this. I admire you all the more. Sometimes we have to lead where no one else has ever been before so we can open up new frontiers. We win only when we think we can, as Dr Logan says, and I believe we can win in this dream for our future. The best success stories are written against the backdrop of challenges that are big enough to really get our attention and release our best effort. That line is not all mine - it came out of what Reginald Palmer said in the meeting when we were first talking about our dreams. This challenge is on that level and awakens our best effort in a game where there are no losers. Everybody wins!

So, thanks, Oscar, so much for coming in to talk with me that day. Now maybe you can catch up on your sleep."

"Maybe," Oscar said. "Right now I am excited about being on your kind of team. I like that phrase, everybody wins! That's the team I want to play on!"

CHAPTER ELEVEN

The Question

"So I have a question I want to ask."

IT WAS SPRINGTIME. AS THE COMPLETION OF THE WORLD CITIZEN Center drew near and the Grand Opening was being planned, Steve was busily engaged in the final details. Beyond that he had a decision to make. The newly formed Board of Directors had asked him to become the official Director of the World Citizen Center. There was one person he wanted to talk to before he made the decision to accept the position.

After church he waited for Sandra to speak to the last person leaving. He came up last at the front door and said, "There's a restaurant in town called the Home at Home Restaurant. We seem to be at home there. But we know about their carry out service and we seem to have another place where we are at home. Could we go up to Dr. Logan's Look Beyond cabin and sit on the deck on this warm day. We could talk about some new details. Could you do that?" Steve asked, smiling as he asked.

"I'm always ready to go up there," Sandra answered openly. "Who is getting the lunch?"

"We'll both get the lunch and then we can ride up together," Steve answered more decisively than usual.

They sat on the deck in what had become a favorite place for them, especially when they could share it together on such a beautiful day.

Following a time of silence, when just being there spoke a new kind of language they seemed to understand more and more, Steve said, "This place up here has been the backdrop for the decision to dream ahead and launch the World Citizen Center. And now that it's coming into being, the Board of Directors has asked me to become it's full time Director. I thought this would be a good place to discuss it together."

"You have been asked to be the Director!" Sandra exclaimed. "That's wonderful. I had heard that, by the grapevine, but you hadn't told me about it"

"I know," Steve said quietly. "I only got the invitation this week. I chose to wait before I said anything so we could talk about it up here where both of us have sat and dreamed the future. Now, the future is here. Tell me, what do you think?"

"I can't answer that," Sandra said. "It's your decision."

"I know. Maybe it is. But, then, maybe it isn't. Maybe it should be our decision," Steve said in response.

"I am not sure why it should be our decision. Why is that the case?" Sandra quizzed.

"I have been thinking about it all week. But there is something else I have been thinking about, longer than a week. And I wanted to talk to you about that up here where we have spent so many hours dreaming about the future. All week I have been thinking in terms of the future being, our future. Together. So I have a question I want to ask. And I want to ask it while we are up here overlooking the valley where we have dreamed together."

Steve took Sandra's hand and led the way as they walked over to the handrail of the deck. Turning toward Sandra, he took both of her hands in his as he said, "In so short a time I have come to love you very much. I have enough reason to believe it may be mutual and that I can ask you a very special question. Sandra Millan, will you marry me?"

Sandra looked at Steve as though the idea was not at all that new. She looked into his eyes and said softly and with emotion, "It's mutual. I love you too, Steve. Very much. And the answer is, yes. Yes, Steve, I will marry you!"

In the silence that followed their kisses, they put their arms around each other and stood together, looking out over the valley below.

CHAPTER TWELVE

Grand Opening

I believe the World Citizen Center will be a great umbrella
under which we can choose a knowledge-based faith
that overarches our politics, religion and respective cultures
as a new giant leap forward for mankind.

THE GRAND OPENING FOR THE WORLD CITIZEN CENTER WAS THE biggest day in Alpine in a long time. Not only was the event announced in the local papers, but in newspapers of nearby cities. In the town paper of Alpine a picture of the World Citizen Center stretched across the front page. The announcement of OPENING DAY was followed by a statement of it's mission. "The World Citizen Center will be a platform where renowned speakers come to present leading-edge knowledge, linked with science and technology, and the Big Ten Universal Qualities."

It's paradigm changer," the writer announced. "It overarches religion so that it is a faith for all the world's people, no matter where they live or what their religion, politics, or culture may be."

Below the full view picture of the grand World Citizen Center, another picture showed Steve Kelly opening the center's front door. It described him as the director who would be bringing in outstanding speakers, especially persons from the universities and research centers, along with cultural and social leaders, all under the framework of the Big Ten Universal Qualities. Steve was quoted, "While the facility of the World Citizen Center will be important to Alpine as a place for many area events, it will make its biggest contribution by giving the people in this area the advantage of hearing outstanding educators, business, and social leaders who give updates on major studies and research findings which are leading indicators of the future, under an umbrella theme of being world class citizens defined by the Big Ten Universal Qualities."

Looking up at the World Citizen Center from the tree lined parking lot created a feeling in character with arriving at the Kennedy Center in Washington, DC. Just to the left of the front entrance stood a tall eloquent contemporary white steel frame of three triangles, shadowed by three towering white pylons. If one chose to expand their representative symbolism, the triple monoliths might suggest Faith, Science, and the Future. To someone else they might suggest Science, Technology, and Universal Qualities! Together they stood as majestic towers to the oneness of all existence.

Paralleling a long patio, the building's front wall was formed by series of tall lightly tinted windows, in units of three, intersected by three flat-sided pilasters of light tan marble, reaching up to a shadowed light tan border at the top.

Inside, and matching the length of the outside patio, a series of skylights stretched above an expanse of blue carpet, giving the gathering space a sense of elegance, while it hushed the sound of people talking as they gathered. Lounge chairs and coffee tables, placed in conversational arrangement in the atrium invited people to gather early for events to share in an exchange of ideas and friendship. It provided people with a feeling of uplift and distinction, all in keeping with what the center was designed to encourage - a new sense of oneness and great hope for the earth family.

Guests with a special invitation to the grand opening included in the bishop of the Triangle Conference, the president of Sagan University, the president of Alpine Tech, key leaders in the Marshall Research Laboratory, and many local business leaders. Civic and education leaders were among the array of excited guests. Included among those who had been invited by special invitation, were those who had made major contributions to a newly formed World Citizen Center Foundation. Even though the venture was supported by a multi million dollar grant from the Vision Foundation that Dr. Logan headed, a local funding program had given people a chance to be a part of making the World Citizen Center into a reality.

Who would be the keynote speaker for the grand opening event? Enthusiastic consensus focused on Dr. James Kelly, whose books had been the inspiration for the dream of creating the unique conference center.

When Steve talked with his granddad about being the keynote speaker, he quietly and respectfully declined. "Steve," he said, in his always respectful manner, "while I am greatly honored by the invitation, there is a better choice. Having me to speak would represent a reference to the past more than a vision from the future."

Steve's granddad explained further. "Dr. David Logan has already ventured the idea of my being the opening speaker, because my books inspired the dream that has become the World Citizen Center. I gave Dr. Logan the same response I am giving you - that the opening speaker should represent a bold new vision from the future.

So, Steve, while I am deeply honored and pleased to be considered for the keynote address, no such special recognition is needed. The years are marching on for me, and I want to honor the future, not the past. So, Steve, with deep appreciation for the consideration, here is my request. You are to give the opening address. I have given considerable thought to this and have already indicated this idea to Dr. Logan. He graciously accepted my explanation. So, Steve, on behalf of the Board of Directors, Dr. Logan will be inviting you to be the keynote speaker. That's as it should be. He knows that you are the one who must carry the banner now. When I told him of my decision, he asked if I would be there and be willing to be recognized. I said that, along with my wife Maria, I would be there and be willing to stand for a moment. So, Steve, you and Dr. Logan, along with Dr. Sandra, have led the vision to its launch point. Now you must lead the way forward."

Before a packed house, Dr. Sandra walked to the center of the platform on the day of the Grand Opening and paused at the speakers podium. She said with excitement, "This is a day of new beginning! We all eagerly await the opening words of Dr. David Logan, whose reach for new tomorrows began this vision. Then we will listen with great interest to the keynote address that Steve Kelly, our Director and leader, will give. But the proper beginning for the opening of the World Citizen Center is with a prayer of thanksgiving from all of us! Bishop Earl Watson is here today and will lead us in our celebration of thanksgiving.

Before Bishop Watson comes to express our collective voice for thanks, I want to talk about the significance of his being here.

Bishop Watson has been an enthusiastic supporter of the dream that we are celebrating today. That support represents how much he believes that while the church must continually care about the broken edges of society, it must also be engaged in an intentional ministry to the minds of vision leaders who can guide us to our best tomorrows. These leaders may live anywhere, but what is unique about them is that they have chosen the identity markers of the Big Ten Universal Qualities to define their place in the human story. These are a voice of the future calling for a new era of oneness for the human family. I am so pleased Bishop Earl Watson is here today to represent that call from the future! 'Bishop Watson, would you come now and lead all of us to enter a prayer of thanksgiving for this new ministry to the mind and call from the future.'"

The distinguished manner in which Bishop Watson walked to the center of the platform indicated a high respect for the significance of the grand opening. When he stood at the podium he paused a moment and said simply, "May we all bow our heads together and pause to recognize the long progression of humanity's progression of faith that has led to this momentous next step forward.'

He began his prayer, saying, 'O Master Teacher of Galilee, we seek now to take our place in your call to a kingdom of dreams, focused anew in the mission of the World Citizen Center. May this be a place where your teachings continue to lead the way to building a new and better humanity.

> O Carpenter of Nazareth, Builder of life divine,
> Who shapest man to God's own law, Thyself the
> fair design:
> Build us a tower of Christ-like height,
> That we the land may view,
> And see like Thee, our noblest work
> Our Father's work to do.
>
> O Thou who dost the vision send
> And givest each his task,
> And with the task sufficient strength:
> Show us Thy will, we ask;
> Give us a conscience bold and good;
> Give us a purpose true,
> That it may be our highest joy,
> Our Father's work to do. [1]

Amen.'"

---

[1] J T Stockings

As Bishop Watson returned to his seat on the platform there was a respectful moment before it seemed right for anyone to move or say anything. It was time for silent thanksgiving for how much this moment in history was a vital part of the new sacred.

Slowly Sandra returned to the podium and turned toward Bishop Watson and said, "Thank you, Bishop Watson."

Facing the audience again, she proclaimed with energized excitement, "This is a day of new beginning! This marks a new day for the town of Alpine, for this region, and for multiple faith communities of the world family to honor the sunrise of new tomorrows.

I now have the privilege of presenting the person whose journey of faith reached such a level of disappointment with the paradigms of yesterday that he was searching for a pathway to a better tomorrow. The disparity between ideas locked in yesterday, and a vision for a greater tomorrow led him to immerse himself in the writings of Dr. James Kelly. Central in Dr. Kelly's books is the premise that choosing the Big Ten Universal Qualities as an identity template can be a framework that updates the ideals of the Master Teacher's Sermon on the Mount to our time in the history.

I am privileged to present a person who dared to believe in those ideals and dreams enough to do something in keeping with Martin Luther's thesis nailed to the church door. Without that person's bold vision we would not be here today, celebrating the grand opening of the World Citizen Center. Join me in welcoming this generous vision leader who matched dreams with resources and action. Please welcome Dr. David Logan!"

Amid the wave of a standing applause, Dr. Kelly walked quickly with excitement to the speakers lectern. "Thank you, Dr. Sandra. And thanks to all of you whose presence here is a celebration of our faith and new beginnings.

My words will be few. I want to put today's event into a larger perspective. In a real sense this quest began when the people of the World Citizen Church and its minister so honored the teachings of Jesus that they dared to change their name to the World Citizen Church, and, in turn, dared to put an icon of that Master Teacher on the altar of their church. My esteem and admiration for those forward thinking people is immense! Now they have chosen to expand that vision by supporting the dream of having a World Citizen Center as a way of re-setting the kingdom of heaven dream in a new age. That is the paradigm we seek to advance in our magnificent World Citizen Center! It's a vision in which, the call from the future is more important than mandates from the past. It is a call serve the present age and make a better world by being better people!

So many of you here today have been a part of this venture where the commanding challenge and vision is to align our faith, science, and technology in an open-ended progression to our best tomorrows.

We have come together here in this banquet hall to celebrate what may be one of the world's most unique centers for defining the future that we ask for. It is a reach for new and greater possibilities in the greatest age the human family has ever known. It's time to celebrate the future in terms of new sunrise dreams, where we have the ongoing challenge to match our best dreams with our growing potential.

I am amazed at the flow of events that have allowed me to be a part of this moment when we are advancing our best hopes and dreams forward. In its own way, this is our "one small step for man; one giant leap for mankind." I believe the World Citizen Center will be a great umbrella under which we can choose a knowledge-based faith that overarches our politics, religion and respective cultures as a new giant leap forward for our earth family.

So, what I have now is, the privilege of presenting to you the young man, who has led the creation of this center during these months of planning and action, and the one who will lead us into the next level of being world citizens on location right here in Alpine. I ask you to welcome a young man who has poured his heart into this daring effort and given voice to dreams that expand the promise of the future. At so young an age, he has led us with remarkable skill. As he leads the way in our reach for a better tomorrow than yesterday, I ask you to greet and welcome your Director of the World Citizen Center, Steve Kelly!

Steve moved quickly to the speakers lectern, then paused and stood there a moment amid the burst of applause. As the applause diminished, Steve began by saying, "I stand on tall shoulders. I stand on the shoulders of people who have dared to live by tall dreams. Today I am a part of a dream that so many of you here are helping to make real!

When we reflect on the long progression of those who have advanced humanity's best thinking, I think of the writer of the book of *Proverbs*. One of Solomon's proverbs says, "*The intelligent man is always open to new ideas. In fact, he looks for them.*"

One of the persons who was open to new ideas, and who stands tallest in the wise man's hall of fame is Jesus of Nazareth. The influence of his life has exceeded that of any other person in the human story, and his story continues to our time. It was Jesus who dreamed of a kingdom of heaven on earth.

We are here today to update that vision, now extended in the Big Ten Universal Qualities, as our call to new beginnings.

One of the persons whose writings have had a significant influence in extending that dream in our time is here today. He dared to believe in turning old endings into new beginnings and write about it.

We all know that Dr. James Kelley is one of those "open to new ideas" persons. I was privileged to hear some of those stories he put in his writing as I sat on the farmhouse porch along with my young adult cousins. All the while, our kind and gracious grandmother,

Maria, kept us supplied with tea and cookies. I am honored to represent the James and Maria Kelly family today. Their three children and all the grandchildren are here today for this event.

When one of today's leading-edge thinkers read Dr. Kelly's stories, he also was looking for new ideas. Out of his disappointment with old yesterday paradigms, Dr. David Logan dared to come to Alpine and share his dream ideas with, Dr. Sandra Millan, his minister at World Citizen Church.

After they talked, I was invited to join them for a meeting on the deck of Dr. Logan's Look Beyond cabin on the peaks of Eagles View Mountain. Our search was to see what we could do to advance the world citizen dream in our time and place. As we looked down over the town of Alpine, those ideas began to come together in a plan which has now become this World Citizen Center! Many other people joined the dream and are here today in this extensive banquet hall, ready to open the conference center as a place where we can be a part a new journey of dreams for new tomorrows.

Although none of the people involved in making this World Citizen Center a reality seek praise or recognition, there are two people here today, without whose nobility of ideas and vision, we would not be here today. We want to say a special Thank You to them now. It was their request that they have no more recognition than what I now request that we respectively give. I speak of James and Maria Kelly, and ask them to please stand as we salute them with an applause of respect and thanks!"

When the long applause ended, Steve said, "Among others who have had such a leading part of making this day possible are Dr. David Logan and Dr. Sandra Milan. Even though both of them have already stood before you today, I ask that Dr. David Logan and Dr. Sandra Milan stand now to receive our gratitude for their place in this wonderful story.

Among those who have served generously of their time and ideas are the leading-edge people of the World Citizen Church,

and the visionary Board of Directors of the World Citizen Center. I
would like for all of them to stand and give us a moment to express
our thanks in a collective applause of appreciation!"

After the series of swelling applause turned into a hushed and
waiting silence, Steve began to address the full audience.

"In our time in history we are beneficiaries of the dreams of
those who have linked our humanity in a new search for common
cause, world citizenship, and new tomorrows. We live in that time
when we have a new and special opportunity to join the heroes of
yesterday, in a link with new heroes, who will advance our best
dreams to new and higher levels of unity and oneness. This is our
time in the long sweep of civilization to look ahead and be a part
of a future worthy of our place in the progression of that story up
to this amazing time in history. It's here we have a place in the
story where we can dream our best dreams and give them their
best chance to happen.

Our time in history is a time when many ages are now rolled
into one. It's the global age, the digital age, the neurological age,
and the age of the computer and its cloud of information, the
technological age. Each new generation of technology rapidly out-
paces the previous one. Some have called this time in which we
are privileged to live the geometric age, where one advance leads
to multiple new advances. As these ages may be folding together
in a new collective intelligence, this is a strategic time when wise
people can dream a great dream for our future as the world family.

I came to Alpine to write my thesis. I brought along some
books and magazines which describe the latest progression of insights for our rapidly changing times. What I am discovering is
that by the time I think I am catching up, I also discover that I
have just gotten behind again. What you have designed here in
the World Citizen Center is a center for open-ended dreams that
can help us to catch up, keep up, and to lead the march forward to
enter a bold, wholesome, and sustainable request of life for our best

future. We have an opportunity to live by a template of The Big Ten Universal Qualities that will lead and sustain our best identity for many generations. These qualities will continue to guide our purpose and programs here at our World Citizen Center so that, far into tomorrow, they will awaken what president Lincoln called, the better angels of our nature.

This, then, is our time and opportunity to make these world class qualities into real time daily living, right here in Alpine, as a guiding framework for how we see the world and our place in it. It's our time to chose those leading-edge qualities which can be chosen by any person, any time, and any place in the world and make them a real part of who we are. That understanding is the platform and mission of the World Citizen Center.

Being a part of this vision has taken over the writing of my dissertation which I came here to write. But I have no regrets. I can finish the thesis while we are all working together to make this center into a place where we can advance the goal of serving the common good of our world family as world citizens.

I had thought to incorporate the latest in psychological theory in my writing. What I am discovering is that I see theory actually being put into practice, not in multiple clinical trials so much as in a clinical trial of one person at a time, living out a story that becomes anecdotal evidence of the power of our dreams. We are engaged in a journey in which the power of the brain to rewrite its guiding instructions, is a dynamic, real time, ongoing process. That positive, leading-identity for our sunrise age is embodied in the Big Ten Universal Qualities that any of us can choose for an identity template to input to our brain. The words of the Big Ten become a kind of identity card we carry around with us in our self-image. Hence, the brain is continually learning and rewriting this image of ourselves as an inspiring guide to our best future. These qualities of kindness and caring, honesty and respect, of collaboration and tolerance, fairness and integrity, and of diplomacy and nobility, are defining words of our ID card that we can, not just to carry around, but make real here in everything we do. We will bring in those future vision speakers who can help us to honor this progression of knowledge which combines our science and technology with the defining qualities of the Big Ten Universal Qualities. These become a call from the future as the new sacred. These will help us take our place in the unfinished dreams of the Master Teacher!

Today we can celebrate a time of new beginning for all of us as we share in the opening of the World Citizen Center. All of us now have an opportunity to enjoy fellowship together in a grand opening reception. In our atrium area, and the parallel patio area, we have prepared refreshments for all. We invite you to share with each other in those areas to make this a time to celebrate together!

But let that follow a special ribbon cutting ceremony. We have some people here who are prepared to stretch a long ribbon all across the stage of this beautiful banquet hall. As they now unroll that ribbon, we are asking some people to help cut the Grand Opening Ribbon.

Dr. and Mrs. James Kelly, may we now have the honor of your coming to the stage so each of you can use one of these oversize scissors to help us cut the ribbon. And Dr. David Logan, would you join them to take part in cutting the ribbon. And as minister of the World Citizen Church, Dr. Sandra Millan would come and be a part of this occasion, and represent the people of the World Citizen Church. There are so many others who have helped make this day possible that we cannot include them all. But, Bishop Earl Watson, bishop of the Triangle Conference of many churches, would you join us here.

And now, with our oversize scissors in hand, let us cut the ribbon to declare that the World Citizen Center is NOW OPEN TO HELP US GIVE OUR BEST DREAMS THEIR BEST CHANCE TO HAPPEN!

CHAPTER THIRTEEN

Wedding Plans!

"We want our wedding ceremony to express respect."

PLANNING THEIR WEDDING WAS EXCITING FOR SANDRA AND STEVE. They met at their favorite site for dreaming, on the peak of Eagles View Mountain. A cold wave sent the thermometer down to near freezing, so Steve and Sandra sat inside Dr. Logan's Look Beyond cottage sharing the warmth of the fireplace. The plans they began to put together defined a wedding ceremony which would honor their sacred commitment to each other as respectful partners, but do so in much different words from the traditional ceremony.

There was no question about who they both wanted to lead the ceremony, Dr. James Kelly. "Let's get on the speaker phone," Sandra said with excitement "and ask your granddad if he will lead the ceremony."

When Grandmother answered the phone, Steve said, "Grandmother, we have some exciting news and we wonder if Granddad could get on the phone, too."

When both of them were on the phone, Grandmother said, "We're both here now and we are listening. What's the good news? Is it what I think it might be?"

"That depends on what you think it might be," Steve answered, "But if you think it is that Sandra and I are going to get married, Sandra gets to be the one to tell that."

"Yes, that's it." Sandra responded with excitement. "And we hope you will be at our wedding and that Dr. Kelly will be the one who officiates."

In her excitement Maria didn't even think about when it would be. She just said immediately, "You can be sure we'll be there! Oh, I am so pleased. Congratulations!"

"Thank you, Grandmother," Steve said. "So I have a question for Granddad. 'Granddad, would you officiate at the wedding, and could Sandra and I come to the farm and meet on the farmhouse porch to plan an updated wedding ceremony?'"

"There is nothing I would like better," Granddad answered with enthusiasm. "And could my bride of many years be a part of this farmhouse porch meeting?" he asked.

"That's very next question I was going to ask. 'Grandmother, could you be a part of this planning time? You and Granddad have modeled what I hope our marriage can be like. Sandra and I want to have the kind of respect for each other that the two of you have. You have held each other in high esteem and are high in our respect and admiration.'"

"I will be so honored," Grandmother responded in an obvious irony, "if you can talk your Granddad into doing the ceremony."

"Oh, I'll do that!" Granddad cut in. "You don't even need to ask. Just give me enough time to say, yes. Yes, indeed!"

"Granddad," Steve said, "we want our wedding ceremony to be different and we wonder if you would be open to that. Of course, I don't wonder very much. I remember our talking one day about creating wedding ceremonies that honor the Big Ten Universal Qualities as the backdrop against which couples make their vows to each other. You said that a ceremony should be less steeped in history and more aligned with those important qualities which make any marriage successful. So we want to ask if we could draft a new ceremony and then, when we get together on the porch, put it all together with ideas both of you may have?"

"I think you already know the answer," Granddad said. "Let's do just that. It will be a high privilege for us!"

And could we meet in the summertime when the kudzu will be in full bloom? And Grandmother, could you bring out some tea and cookies." Steve asked.

"Oh, yes, indeed," Grandmother answered immediately, connecting memories with earlier porch-story days.

As the four of them gathered on the porch, Sandra said, "I can see why this place holds such vivid memories. Steve speaks of it as though it were an epiphany. And now I know why. I am so privileged to be a part of it."

"More than just a part of it," Granddad said warmly. "We already consider you our granddaughter. Maria and I love welcoming you to the porch and into the Kelly family!

As they relaxed on the porch, Granddad said, "Thanks for emailing me your ideas. I have already read through your proposed ceremony two times. It reflects not only your love and mutual respect, but it is a ceremony that can be used for future ceremonies where a partnership of dreams binds two person's stories together in new beginnings. I am so very pleased. No changes are needed. It's just right, and ready for the time when Maria and I will be so pleased to be a part of it on your special day of new beginnings!"

"Sandra and I are highly honored that both of you can be a part of our dreams," Steve said. He reached over and took Sandra's hand and squeezed it gently while she squeezed back.

"But there's one more thing," Sandra said. "I have a question for you, Dr. Kelly, to which I hope you will say, yes. Dr. Kelly, I mean, Granddad. Granddad, we want you to be the guest minister at the worship service the morning of our wedding day. Could you add that to your part in our special day?"

"That doesn't require much thinking for me to give you an

answer," Granddad said. "I would be pleased to have that opportunity! When will it be?"

"Sandra can answer that," Steve said.

"Well, I can hardly wait that long," Sandra responded, "but it will be deep in September, September twenty-four. Would that time work for both of you?"

Grandmother answered eagerly. "I am sure we can make it work."

"We can, indeed," Granddad added.

CHAPTER FOURTEEN

Wedding Day Service

*We are all privileged to live in the greatest time in all human history.
It's a great time to talk about the Big Ten
Universal Qualities as the new sacred.*

As the worship service at the World Citizen Church began, Dr. Sandra followed the choir as they processed into the chancel, then went on down from there to the center of the chancel to share greetings. The sanctuary was crowded. The time of greetings and fellowship followed the usual pattern of visiting with the people and asking them to introduce visitors. She said, "Since there are likely to be so many visitors here today, I ask that you keep your introductions a little shorter than usual. Why so many people? It couldn't have anything to do with who our guest minister is today, could it? Oh, it could," she said, as if they had said, 'yes.' I join all of you in recognizing this as a very special day for us to share our faith and affirmations together."

After Dr. Sandra completed the greetings and fellowship moments, she turned and went to the speakers lectern where she said, "Let us follow the Call to Worship and Learning, as printed in the bulletin. Let's join together as we say,

From our many walks of life, we now join in cele-
bration of our faith.
We have already experienced the wonders of nature as
we drove through the tree-lined streets of our town.
We respect our place in the mystery of all existence.
We respect our place in the earth's lengthening story.
We respect our place in the human family's story.
We reach anew for the inspiration that helps us to
be the best we can be in our time in history and
place in the story.

Now let us join in singing, "This Is a Day of New Beginnings."

When it came time for the sermon, Sandra stood at the speakers lectern and said, "I have the distinct privilege of introducing the person who will introduce our guest minister this morning. I think it may be no secret that the person I now introduce to introduce our speaker is soon to be my husband, Steve Kelly.

"Steve," she said in amused tones, I think you know our speaker, so will you come now and introduce him as our distinguished speaker for today."

When Steve came to the speakers lectern he said, "Thank you, Sandra. I do know our speaker. I have known him many years. I call him Granddad. He is Dr. James Kelly.

Many of you may know him by way of reading his writings, which were so significant in the vision to extend our ministries into the World Citizen Center. As we welcome him, we also especially welcome his wife, Maria Kelly, whom I, and now Sandra call, Grandmother. We are so honored to have them here.

I now have the high privilege of presenting to you our distinguished guest speaker today, Dr. James Kelly."

Dr. Kelly came up from the audience and stepped respectfully up to the pulpit. He began by saying, "Maria and I are highly honored to be here on this very special day for Steve and Sandra. And I treasure having this high privilege of speaking in your church where our new granddaughter, Sandra, whom you respectfully call, Dr. Sandra, interprets a knowledge-based, open-ended faith here week after week.

The long development of faith in the human family took a great leap forward in the life and teachings of Jesus. When Matthew gave an account of how great crowds began to follow Jesus to hear him teach, he wrote in his biography, "One day as the crowds were gathering, he went up the hillside with his disciples and sat down and taught them there."

I had heard about it, but I hadn't seen it until I walked into your sanctuary yesterday and there it was. Instead of a cross on the altar, speaking about the death of Jesus, there it was, a representation of Jesus, with people standing around listening to Jesus as a the Master Teacher. I stopped and just stood there in admiration. I thought to myself, '*that's as it should be!*' We've made to much of the death of Jesus and not enough of his life and teachings. This representation on your altar says a lot about this church and its willingness to think of our faith as an ongoing progression to be lived out in our world in our time.

When the people of his own time tried to figure out Jesus, some thought of him as the new Moses. But Jesus assured his listeners that he wasn't trying to reinforce the Ten Commandments, about what not to do. Instead, he wanted to help them know what to do to build a new kingdom of love and understanding. He didn't talk about how to correct yesterday, so much as about, how to create tomorrow. It was not about converting people to religion, but helping people build a faith for a better life and better world.

That world is in a rapid state of change in our time. Leading visionaries are projecting our future, saying that we will have technologically enhanced minds and bodies, assisted by robots and computers, that will make us smarter than we have ever been before. They are projecting cures for debilitating diseases like Alzheimer's and diabetes, prosthesis controlled by thoughts, brains that rewrite their own instructions for recovery after debilitating strokes, replacement organs and parts, genes that replace defective genes, all of which can extend life expectancy to one hundred years and beyond.

Great as that is, that is not enough. The need for our time is for new leaders, whose vision of the future guides us to the best human qualities ever dreamed. That's why it is important to have that statuette of Jesus as the Master Teacher on the altar of your church. We need the unfinished dreams of this "kingdom of heaven teacher" to walk among the pathways of our minds and appear in our dreams so that we can find our way to a higher humanity in the greatest age the human family has ever known.

I have been trying to take a queue from both Moses and Jesus. So, I have borrowed the number from Moses, and the directions from Jesus. I want to talk about the Big Ten Universal Qualities as the new sacred. I like to believe the teachings of Master Teacher are condensed in the Big Ten Universal Qualities – that they embody what Jesus was trying to teach when he walked on the dusty roads from Nazareth to Jerusalem, and when he asked his followers to, "Go and make disciples in all the nations." An echo of that call sounds anew from the statuette of the Master Teacher on your altar in this World Citizen Church.

Today I want to focus on one of the words of the Big Ten – integrity.

Integrity is not that easiest word to talk about, so let me begin by telling you, in a kind of parallel to the parables of Jesus, about the overalls we wore as country boys. They got holes in them, mostly at the knees, so my mother would patch them and then, when the patches got holes in them, she patched the patches, until finally, when they were just too worn out to patch, she would go to the bargain basement at a department story and get me a new pair for ninety-nine cents, or something like that. Those old overalls were different from the ones teenagers just have to have in our time, you know, the ones that already have holes in the knees when they buy them new, for closer to ninety-nine dollars than ninety-nine cents. But the holes in those boyhood overalls were real. Authentic. Genuine. Those overalls had integrity.

People with integrity are highly valued people in our high tech aged. In the same sense, churches that highlight integrity are equally important. And having integrity in either of those categories is not easy to achieve. So I highly respect the level of integrity I sense here. How many churches do you know who have written the Big Ten Universal Qualities into their mission statement and their program ministry? How many churches have had the insight to represent Jesus, as the Master Teacher on their altar? And do you know how many churches there are in the world who would dare to change their name to World Citizen Church? I know of just one, and I marvel that I am standing here in that one church now.

I am flattered when people say that my books have inspired you to extend your ministry by creating the World Citizen Center. And, I can hardly believe the coincidence that my grandson just happened to be here while all this was happening and met and fell in love with the minister of this church. So what makes Maria and me so very proud is that we get to be a part the wedding of our grandson and our newest granddaughter.

I am quite sure you already know there is to a wedding here this afternoon. Steve and Sandra are going to get married here in this church just a few hours from now. And I am going to be privileged to lead their marriage ceremony. And, as you might expect, we are going to depart from the traditional ceremony. They have written their own vows which incorporate the Big Ten Universal Qualities into the commitments they make to each other as real time expectations of themselves.

The wedding itself is by invitation, since the church would not begin to seat all who would like to attend. But the reception at the World Citizen Center is open on a come-and-go basis.

Maria and I will be there and look forward to meeting and talking with as many of you as will come up to us and give us that privilege.

Dr. Kelly looked over at Steve, sitting near the front and said, "Steve, how long have you been studying up on Eagles View?"

"More than two years," Steve answered.

"And how long have you known Sandra?"

"About the same length of time."

"And how long have you been in love with Sandra?"

"From the day I first met her!" Steve answered, gladly.

Dr. Kelly closed out the little interview, saying, "whatever the length of time, I am so pleased that the two of you found each other. We are pleased to be a part of this event which includes this worship service."

I have been a part of the World Future Society for many years. One of its leading purposes is to help us see our place in a larger perspective of time and place. One year the World Future Annual conferences was in San Francisco. As part of building larger perspectives, participants are invited to be a part of a tour to some nearby place of interest. The tour for that particular year was to go out to the amazing Yosemite National Park. Just beyond the back of the grand Ahwahnee hotel, six of us who had been good friends across many years and from many places, took chairs out to the edge of the little lake there. We arranged our chairs so we could see Half Done, that grand marvel of stone created by glaciers long, long ago. That symbol of millions of years of time was reflected in the little lake in front of us. Intentionally, we sat there and referenced our time in history and place in the story to the time frame represented by Half Done.

When one measures by that marker of time, the whole human story only gets a tiny second on the Half Dome clock of time. We were aware that the six of us sitting there barely had a micro second on that clock. It's a very humbling comparative index. And now, in that micro second, we have arrived on stage in the digital-molecular age.

Half Dome is a convergence of molecules. We are a convergence of molecules. With our new tools of science and technology we are learning that both Half Done, and each of us, is a part of endless expressions of the atoms of molecules. I can't explain how it happens. I will leave that to the physicists and astrophysicists. But beyond all that, what all of us, scientist or lay persons, can do, is to marvel at the ultimate mystery of our existence and make our time and place in the story one that honors the best we can be in the lengthening story of people on planet earth.

We are all privileged to live in the greatest time in all human history to be led by the sunrise paradigms from the future, rather than be pushed by sunset paradigms from the past. We have reached a new turning point. We have a chance to live in a partnership with the amazing products of our science and technology, linked to universal qualities which will help to increase our alliance with the grand oneness of all existence.

The words of the Big Ten Universal Qualities form an overarching identity template that gives us our best chance to be world citizens. The more any of us build those words into our identity, the more we expand the potential of the whole family to be winners in our new age of marvel and respect framed by the words of the Big Ten Universal Qualities.

The words of the Big Ten are the defining words Steve and Sandra have chosen to be central in their wedding day commitments to each other. Steve and Sandra will stand before a representation of the Master Teacher and make their commitments to each other defined by the personal qualities of Kindness, Caring, Honesty, and Respect, by the relationship qualities of Collaboration, Tolerance, Fairness, and Integrity; and by the summit qualities of Diplomacy and Nobility.

These ten words become an updated call from the Master Teacher to take up his unfinished dream in our own story. When, one by one, the human family lives by the defining markers of the Big Ten Universal Qualities, they will enable us to have parallels to "footsteps on the moon" and "one giant leap for mankind."

We have been to school in thousands of years of history and have progressed enough from the cave up to our time when we now have the marvelous new tools of science, technology, and the Big Ten qualities that we can use in achieving magnificent sunrise tomorrows. If, and when, we merge these gifts of our hands and minds into a call from the future, we will be marching in step with the Master Teacher!

One of the persons who heard the Master Teacher speaking from the mountainside long ago must have sensed the magnificence of the moment and wrote about it, both in the worldview of his time and against a backdrop on the mystery of the oneness of all existence. So he wrote:

> *And there in the same country shepherds abiding in the fields, keeping watch over their flock by night. And, lo, the angel of the Lord came upon them, and the glory of the Lord shone around about them: and they were sore afraid, And the angel said unto them, Fear not: for behold, I bring you good tidings of great joy, which shall be to all people. For unto you is born this day in the city of David a Saviour, which is Christ the Lord. And this shall be a sign unto, Ye shall find the babe wrapped in swaddling clothes, lying in a manger. And suddenly there was with the angel a multitude if the heavenly host praising God, and saying, Glory to God in the highest, and on earth peace, good will toward men.* Luke 2:8-14 KJV

Dr. Kelly bowed his head slightly for only a moment of thoughtful silence and then quietly said, "Amen."

Sandra moved slowly to the speakers lectern and said, "In the magnanimity of that story then, and now, "Let's all stand together and join in an Affirmation of Faith.

> **I will make the personal qualities of kindness, caring, honesty, and respect, the markers by which I measure my story.**

> **I will make the relationship qualities of collaboration, tolerance, fairness, and integrity, into the ways I live and work with others.**

> **I will make the summit qualities of diplomacy and nobility, the hallmark of my quest to define who I am trying to be.**

> **This quest will exceed and be greater than any of my failures. I will continue to picture myself as I want to be.**

> **I will announce myself to that quest as part of a long reach and many new beginning places.**

> **I will respect the oneness of all existence and do my best to honor that in my place in the story as my request of life.**

CHAPTER FIFTEEN

The Wedding

"I ask of you to wear this ring, as a daily reminded,
of our sacred commitment to each other as faithful partners."

STEVE HAD BEEN SO DEEPLY INVOLVED IN THE CREATING THE WORLD Citizen Center that Dr. Logan asked him to continue to live in his Look Beyond cottage on Eagles View Mountain until after the wedding and the time when he would move into the parsonage where Sandra lived. In an email to Steve, he said, " I know it will not be quite as ideal as being up there in the Spring and Summer, but as the Artist of Autumn paints its review of colors across the sweeping landscape there will be some compensation for the cold and snow of winter."

Winter turned to springtime and summer and into fall. Steve and Sandra now met on Eagle View more often than before and enjoyed making plans for their wedding day. There was little doubt as to where the wedding would be. It would be at the World Citizen Church.

In the sanctuary of the World Citizen Church, two large arrangements of flowers stood on each side of the altar, accenting the distinction of the statuette of the Master Teacher.

Soft organ music quietly filled the church as guests arrived and waited in suspense and respect. A violin and organ duet awakened the emotions of the moment to a higher sense of expectancy. A crescendo in the organ music indicated the beginning of the wedding. Dr. Kelly entered the chancel area and stood to one side so the attention would be on the center aisle. When the organ music swelled to a full crescendo, Sandra and Steve came down the aisle together. In one hand Sandra carried a bouquet of daisies, and with the other she held to Steve's extended arm. When they arrived at the front of the chancel, the music softened, then went silent. Out of the stillness, Dr. Kelly's mellow voice reflected the sacred nature of the occasion.

"Marriage represents a dream, long held by the human family, that two people can merge their stories and future into a partnership of trust, loyalty, and love, and then live more completely together than alone.

Steve and Sandra, you have come to promise to face the future together. You do not know what tomorrow will be like, whether fair or stormy, only that you will face it together in the strength which comes from the love and loyalty you give to each other. This moment is a celebration of your hopes and dreams and a commitment of loyalty to each other. This moment is sacred.

Members of your families are here to give their blessings on your commitments to each other. By standing now, they indicate their continuing faithful support.

When family members took their seats again, Dr. Kelly led the way into the chancel, but again, stood off to one side. Steve and Sandra followed and stood in front of the Master Teacher, represented on the altar. As they stood at the altar it was as though they were among the listening and learners across the expanse of time.

From the side Dr. Kelly said,

There is a oneness in all existence and we are a part of it in our moment in time. Jesus of Nazareth spoke of our place in life's larger setting and its ongoing self-fulfilling forces, when he said, *'While you are asking, and you will be given what you ask for. While you are seeking, and you will find. While you are knocking the door will be opened.'*

In marriage relationships, the words of Jesus are fulfilled again and again in what he said, *"whatever measure you give - large or small - will be used to measure what is given back to you."*

Steve and Sandra, the promises you make to each other are dynamic and circular in that, what you give to life becomes your request of life, and the faithful honor you give to each other will set the respect you may rightfully receive in return. Your promises to each other set new expectations that each of you can honor and live up to as you share the journey of life together.

The words of the Big Ten Universal Qualities can define your gifts to each other and your expectations of each other. The personal qualities are kindness and caring, honesty and respect. The relationship qualities

are collaboration and tolerance, fairness and integrity. The summit qualities are diplomacy and nobility.

When these qualities are built into your identity and your relationships, they will build confidence and reward the trust you place in each other. These qualities can help you to be wholesome, pleasant, and fun persons, so that each of you will find joy and happiness in being with each other. Are these the qualities you pledge to give to each other? If so, answer, Yes.

Yes.

The wedding ring is a timeless symbol of commitment to each other. It is betrayed by dishonesty and selfishness. It is honored by faithfulness and trust.

Steve, will you now give a wedding ring to Sandra that she can wear as a continuing symbol of your promise to love and honor her? If so, place this ring on her finger, and say to her,

Sandra, I ask of you to wear this ring, as a daily reminded of our sacred commitment to each other as faithful partners.

Sandra, will you now give a wedding ring to Steve that he can wear as a continuing symbol of your promise to love and honor him? If so, place this ring on his finger and say,

Steve, I ask of you to wear this ring, as a reminded of our sacred commitment to each other as faithful partners.

Let this be a day of new beginning in a shared journey of love and respect in which the best you give to each other, will be your request of each other, and your noble request of life.

Steve and Sandra, now that you have made commitments to each other for your future together, I am privileged now to announce that you are now partners in marriage.

Steve and Sandra, as you now honor each other with a kiss, let this day of new beginnings lead the way to new sunrise tomorrows.

SEQUELS: New Tomorrows, Apple Blossom Time, The Future We Ask For, A Place In The Story, Eagles View Mountain, Sunrise Dreams, The New Sacred.